THE REMOVERS

No. 3

in the great Matt Helm

suspense series

Don't miss Matt Helm in these bestselling novels of intrigue

"One of the few credible secret agents in today's fiction . . . Helm is a genuinely tough and tough-minded protagonist; your reading diet lacks essential vitamins if you overlook him."

—THE NEW YORK TIMES BOOK REVIEW

the removers

by donald hamilton

A FAWCETT GOLD MEDAL BOOK

FAWCETT PUBLICATIONS, INC., GREENWICH, CONN.

the removers

Chapter One

To GET TO Reno, Nevada, from the southeast, in summer, if you don't have an air-conditioned car, you first sleep all day in Las Vegas. Then you eat a leisurely dinner, waiting for the sun to go down. You pack your gear and head off into the desert, which is cooling off now and bearable, if not exactly frigid. You drive all night through great areas of black nothing. The monotony is broken only by occasional neat signs informing you that the mysterious government installations along the way are none of your business, even if your taxes did help build them.

Then the sun comes up again, and a little while later you're in Reno, ready to get your divorce. I already had mine. I was just looking up my ex-wife, remarried now and living on a ranch somewhere nearby, because for some reason she wanted me to.

After a shower, a shave, and a belated breakfast, I re-read Beth's letter while resting comfortably on one of the twin beds of an air-conditioned motel unit near the Truckee River. They do have a river in Reno, which is more than you can say for Las Vegas; and in other respects it's a little more of a town and a little less of a gold-plated gambling joint. Not that Reno qualifies as a staid and churchly community, by a long shot. No Nevada town does. I couldn't hear the clank of the slot machines from where I lay, but that could have been just because it was still quite early in the day, or because the wind was wrong.

The letter was addressed to Mr. Matthew Helm, since Beth still clung to the notion that a nickname has no place on an envelope. It was written in blue-black ink on good rag paper bearing a cattle brand and the heading: *Double-L Ranch, Middle Fork, Nevada.* It was quite short.

> Dear Matt:
> When we parted, you said that if I or the children should ever need you, you would come.
> I have no right to ask, of course, but we need you now.
>
> > Sincerely,
> > Beth
> > (Mrs. Lawrence Logan)

She'd gone to one of those strict eastern schools, almost vanished from the educational scene, where they still taught such cruel, old-fashioned disciplines as penmanship, regardless of the frustrations and inhibitions that might thereby be produced in the sensitive minds of their helpless charges. Maybe this educational trauma was at the root of her troubles, if you want to call them that. She wouldn't want to. In her view, as was only natural, there was nothing wrong with her. I was the one with troubles—troubles too terrible for a woman to share. Well, we could both be half right.

Anyway, she had a lovely, neat, precise and well-disciplined handwriting that reminded me of the lovely, neat, precise and well-disciplined person from whom it had come. We'd never quarreled; she wasn't someone you could quarrel with. There's not much satisfaction in yelling at someone who won't yell back. We'd even parted company in a quite civilized manner.

"Beth," I'd said, "can't you simply forget about it?"

"No," she'd whispered, "no, I can't forget! How can I?"

I said, "Well, we might as well call it quits, then. I'll take my old pickup truck and the stuff in the studio. You can have the station wagon and the house and all the rest of it. I won't be needing much furniture where I'm going."

She winced and said, "I'm sorry, Matt. I just can't help . . . I'm sorry."

She probably was, but the fact remained that she could no longer bear to have me around. We'd had almost fifteen years, perhaps more than I'd had a right to expect. Then, one day, as I should have known would happen, the war, which I'd fought in a kind of specialized way with some kind of specialized characters, had caught up with me.

I'd had to call into play certain skills and attitudes I'd learned under the tutelage of a gentleman known as Mac, with fairly messy results, which Beth had witnessed. She'd seen the good, gentle Dr. Jekyll turn, briefly, into the nasty, violent Mr. Hyde, and the shock had remained with her. Well, there wasn't much point in forcing a woman to live with a man who turned her stomach; besides, it wasn't much fun for the man.

"I guess Reno's your best bet," I said. "Get a good lawyer and tell him I'll sign anything he wants." I'd hesitated then, not wanting to sound too corny and magnanimous, but it had been a pretty good marriage while it lasted, and I had to admit that the cause of the breakup, strictly speaking, lay in my past, not hers. I said, "It seems unlikely, but if the occasion should ever arise that you or the kids need a man of my peculiar talents, don't hesitate to call on me. After all, I'm still their daddy, no matter what a judge says."

I'd meant it all right, but it was essentially just one of those impressive lines you speak as you go out the door. I hadn't really expected her ever to take me up on it. I'd walked out and headed for the nearest phone and called Mac long distance to let him know I was coming back to work—he'd been after me to do it—after fifteen years of making my living peacefully with typewriter and camera. I'd been in Europe on official government business, never mind what, when notice reached me I was no longer a married man. Now, only some six months later, Beth was asking for help.

She must have found it difficult, I reflected. She must have swallowed a lot of pride to write those few lines.

She hadn't swallowed quite all of it, however. There was that little parenthesis under the signature—*Mrs. Lawrence Logan*—that specified the terms on which I was to come, if I did choose to come, quite clearly. Apparently she wasn't quite desperate enough to summon me as just a woman calling to a man. She wanted to make sure I wouldn't get any wrong ideas. If I helped her, she was saying, I was helping her as another man's wife, take it or leave it.

"Will you go, Eric?" Mac had asked after I'd read the letter the first time, standing by his desk in Washington on my return from Europe. I was always Eric in that office, no matter what names I might use elsewhere.

"Have I a choice?" I asked.

Then I glanced at him sharply. He was a lean, middle-aged man with close-clipped gray hair. He wore a gray flannel suit, and he looked about as much like Madison Avenue as an old gray timber wolf looks like your clipped pet poodle. They have some cold, hard, bright and ruthless men along that street, to be sure, but in one sense they're all thoroughly domesticated. They may talk big about cutting the throats of the opposition, or sticking knives in competitors' backs, but they are speaking quite figuratively, of course. The sight of real blood would send them all screaming for the police.

Blood has never bothered Mac a bit, as far as I know, and he's been responsible for the shedding of a lot of it.

He interpreted my questioning glance correctly. "Yes," he said, "I read the note. As a matter of fact, not knowing where to reach you, Mrs. Logan sent it to me with a covering letter, asking me to look it over and pass it on only if you were not on assignment. There was, she wrote, no point in worrying you if you were not free to come, and she did not wish to interfere with your efficiency, if you were on a dangerous mission. She seems quite a sensible and considerate person in many respects—and quite attractive, too."

"I didn't know you knew my wife—my ex-wife."

He said, "I paid her a visit last fall, while your divorce was still pending. It wasn't good security, of course, but she already knew more about us than she should, after that trouble you had in Santa Fe. Primarily, I wanted to see if she could be trusted to keep quiet, but I did think that perhaps, if I explained the patriotic necessity of your work with us, past and present, she might understand. . . ." He shrugged his shoulders ruefully.

I hadn't known that he'd tried to intercede for me. "It was kind of you to take the trouble, sir."

"A commander must concern himself with whatever affects the morale of his troops," Mac said dryly. "As it turned out, I accomplished nothing in your behalf, quite the contrary. Your wife was very nice, very attentive, and quite horrified. She kept looking me over carefully to see where I kept my horns and tail."

I said, "I've often wondered about that myself, sir." After a moment, I asked, "Did you meet this fellow Logan, the one she later married?"

"Yes, he owns and manages the guest ranch at which she was staying. He seemed pleasant enough; a lean British type with a sandy Air Force moustache. I had a feeling he might be able to take care of himself in a pinch, but it's hard to tell with these understated, expatriate Englishmen. They all make a point of looking as if one could knock them over with a feather, and sometimes one can."

I glanced at the note I was still holding, folded it, and put it in my pocket. "In her covering letter, Beth didn't give you any hint of what kind of difficulty she's in that she expects me to fix up for her?"

"No."

"And it's okay if I take a little time off to investigate?"

He nodded. "You have a vacation coming, Eric." He looked at me over the desk, studying me as if to see if I'd changed in any way since I'd last been in that office. "When you get to Reno, check in at the Riverside Motel," he said. "There'll be a reservation waiting for you." He wrote something on a piece of paper and held it out.

I looked at him hard. "What's this?"

"A contact number in Reno. Agent Paul. Memorize and destroy."

I said dryly, "A vacation, I think you said, sir."

"Paul is quite young and inexperienced. He may need help."

"Doing what?"

"Don't ask unless you really want to know."

I said, "It's his assignment, I gather. If he needs me, he can brief me."

"Precisely," Mac said. "When you've seen him, if you see him, let me know what you think. I don't feel he's going to work out for us. One can't do much with these infants brought up on peace and togetherness." He hesitated. "You can use him if you like, but only if you need assistance badly. Our people have other things to do than look after independent knights-errant on private missions for their ladies fair."

I said, "She's not my lady fair, she's Logan's. She makes that pretty plain."

"She makes it plain," Mac murmured. "Nevertheless, it's you to whom she's turned for help, not Logan. But no doubt that's occurred to you." After a moment, he said, dismissing me: "Don't forget to stop by the recognition room on your way out. There may be some new faces in the files since you left the country."

Chapter Two

THE RECOGNITION ROOM shares the basement of the building with a fancy filing system that was discarded by the FBI or somebody when IBM or somebody sold them a still fancier one. Although technically obsolete, it's good enough for us. We don't have to keep tabs on all the criminals in the world, or even all the spies and secret agents. We just concentrate on the people in our own line of business, and there aren't too many of those. It's an exacting and unrewarding profession, by most standards.

I heard Mac repeat his stock inspirational lecture on the subject last fall before I went overseas. At the time, taking a refresher course of training to make up for my fifteen-year layoff, I was a member of a class of seven bright young things, male and female, all terribly eager to see the top man in the flesh for the first time, and three hard-bitten retreads like myself, all trying to keep from yawning. We'd seen him.

"It's a war of sorts, ladies and gentlemen," Mac had said, standing before us, "and you can consider yourselves soldiers of sorts, but I'd rather you wouldn't. Don't make up any pretty mental pictures. If you were working for a criminal organization, you'd be known as enforcers. Since you're working for a sovereign nation, you can call yourselves . . . well, removers is a very good word. It describes the job with reasonable accuracy. . . ."

I went through the current files carefully, refreshing my memory about my fellow-removers in the services of other countries—the ones known to be operating in the United States, particularly. There were people in the service of friendly nations, who were to be treated with consideration if possible. Of course, it wasn't always possible. There were the small fry of the opposing team, who were merely to be reported if seen. Finally, there were the other side's big guns, as far as we had them spotted. There were Dickman, Holz, Rosloff, Martell, and a deadly female we knew only as Vadya, all with the highest priority. Of these, only one had been reported in the country recently. I frowned and went back through the cards.

"Martell," I said. "I thought he'd dropped out of sight after that Berlin business. Give him to me on the projector, please, Smitty."

Smitty limped to the rear of the room and turned on the machine. He limped because he didn't have much in the way of feet. They had been operated on drastically by some gentlemen in search of information. Various other parts of Smitty were also missing, and there were scars that didn't make him very pleasant to look at.

Mac had given him this job upon his discharge from the hospital, since he was obviously no longer fit for field duty. Don't think for a moment it was just a generous gesture towards a disabled employee. We all had to check with the recognition room before we went out on assignment; we all had to see Smitty therefore, before every job. It was an antidote for optimism and over-confidence, since it was well known that Smitty had been as good as any of us, in his time. He'd just been a little careless, once.

The picture came on the screen. Projecting it didn't help much. If a picture is lousy to start with, blowing it up doesn't improve it—something the TV manufacturers don't seem to have discovered yet. This was just a fuzzy telephoto shot of a man getting out of a car, taken at extreme range by a hidden photographer who should have used a heavier tripod to hold his equipment steady. The printing on the card came through nice and clear, however.

Martell, I read, *Vladimir. 5' 11", 190 lbs., black hair, wide forehead, heavy eyebrows, brown eyes, straight nose, thick lips, strong chin. Fingerprints as Martell not on record, but see below. Expert pistol, poor rifle, adequate*

*knife and unarmed combat. Not known to drink exces-
sively. Not known to use drugs. No known homosexual
tendencies. Officially reprimanded 47 and 50 for attentions to women leading to neglect of duty. Responsible
death Agent Francis in Berlin Sep 51. Unreported
until Feb 60 when seen in Miami Beach acting as bodyguard for Dominic Rizzi, using name Jack Fenn. Found to
have established, under this name, authentic criminal
record dating back to 53 (see reverse for details and fingerprints). Purpose of cover unknown. Current mission
unknown. Present whereabouts unknown. Priority One.*

So they'd found him and lost him; somebody would
have caught hell for that. I frowned at the figure on the
screen. One of the short-range lads; he didn't like a rifle.
A ladies' man; and he must be damn good at his work to
still be in business with two counts of that against him.
His employers weren't noted for leniency towards agents
who goofed off after women.

"Who's Rizzi?" I asked.

"His line was dope, mainly," Smitty said, behind me.
"He's in jail now. He was caught in the Appalachian
roundup of syndicate big-shots."

"That would put Mr. Martell out of a job," I said.
"Well, he shouldn't have much trouble finding himself a
new position. He's spent seven or eight years building
himself a cover as torpedo for the syndicate, judging by
what it says here." I grimaced at the fuzzy image on the
screen. "He's well qualified, you've got to hand him that.
Those gangsters will never hire a better-trained hatchet
man. Let's hope they appreciate him. I just wonder what
the hell he's up to, playing hoodlum."

"So does the man upstairs," Smitty said. "He's been
wearing out that photo, looking at it for inspiration."

"Anything else?" I asked. "No other pix?"

"No, but there's an unconfirmed report on the master
card, here, to the effect that Martell was seen in Reno
recently, carrying a gun for a racketeer named Fredericks.
The report is being investigated, it says here."

I made a wry face at the screen. That was why Mac

had a green kid in Nevada, then, and was asking me to back him up. It would be one of those annoying deals where you're on standby duty simply because you happen to be around. You haven't got anything specific to do, but you can be damn sure that just about the time you're about to turn out the light and go to bed with the girl, the phone will start ringing.

Not that I had a girl in mind—or if I did, she was married to another man, and if I knew her, she'd be taking her marriage vows very seriously. She'd always been a very serious girl.

Chapter Three

WEST OF RENO, they have some quite respectable mountains, as the early emigrants discovered to their dismay, including some folks named Donner, who couldn't manage to beat the snow across, and spent the winter in camp eating each other. There's a monument to them up towards the pass that bears their name. Well, maybe they earned it, but it does seem a little unfair to the better-organized outfits who made it on a regular diet and so missed the opportunity to get their names carved in stone or cast in bronze—I forget the exact material used.

I'd been up that way years before, but this time I swung down along the foothills after leaving the motel. It was close to three in the afternoon when I reached the metropolis of Middle Fork, which consisted of a general store with a gas pump out front. They supplied me with soda pop and directions, said I couldn't possibly miss it; and I proceeded back into the hills.

The little road wound upwards with the usual assortment of bumps, ruts, and unreliable-looking bridges. It forked here and there. Sometimes there were signs pointing to various places, including the ranch I was looking for, but sometimes I had to toss a coin to make the choice. I didn't mind. Washington was far away, with the gray-haired man behind the desk, and the recognition room full of pictures of unpleasant people it was my duty to do something about if I should happen to bump into them.

The old pickup truck was running well, and it was nice, wild, clean country; and if I got lost I'd just heat a can of beans over the gasoline stove I carried, and crawl into my sleeping bag in the rear, under the weatherproof metal canopy, and find my way in the morning.

I came upon the gate quite abruptly. It was a kind of
rustic arch composed of two massive uprights and a long
cross timber that sagged slightly in the middle as they always do after they've been up some time. The Double-L
brand had been carved into the timber, and in case you
were too dumb to figure it out, it was spelled out for
you, too: DOUBLE-L RANCH. On one of the uprights was
a small, weather-beaten metal sign: *Guests*.

I turned in. The road wasn't bad, now, in dry
weather, but I could imagine it would be a real experience
in winter, impassable at times. Coming around a bend, I
found myself on an open shoulder of the mountain with
a view that merited a photograph—I'd brought a camera
along to get some shots of the kids. I got out, and
climbed up the hill to snap the picture. I shoved the
camera into my hip pocket as I started back down.
They've got a new model now that'll feed the baby, walk
the dog, and even take pretty good photographs, but
somehow the notion of a miniature camera as a portable
pocket instrument seems to have got lost along the way.
I still like the little old Leica you can carry in your
pants.

When I reached the road, the first thing I saw was the
horse. It was standing docilely, reins loose and trailing,
just an ordinary brown horse with an ordinary stock
saddle. It did carry a scabbard for a carbine, not unusual
for a ranch. I had time to note that the scabbard was
empty. Then the owner of the horse came around the
rear of the truck with a Winchester .30-30 in his hands
and aimed it at me.

"Put your hands up!" he said.

He was a compact young fellow, I saw, in his early
twenties, dressed about like I was in jeans, boots, a work
shirt, and a big hat. It's the costume of the country, and
I'd changed into it at the motel, not wanting to come to a
family reunion looking too much like a dude. Besides, a
boot-top makes a handy place to carry a revolver if you
don't like holsters—and after all, Beth *had* called for
help. I also had a knife.

"Stop right there!" the kid snapped as I continued

walking towards him. He waved the gun-barrel at me. "I told you to put 'em up."

He was talking too much. He wasn't going to shoot. I could see it in his eyes. I was almost close enough to take the gun away and spank him with it. I don't like fool kids who wave those things in my face.

"Peter!" somebody called from up the slope. "Pete, where. . . ? Oh, there you are!" There was a little pause, and then, "Why, it's Matt!"

I recognized the voice. It wasn't surprising. I'd lived with it for better than a dozen years, once—pretty good years, at that.

"What in heaven's name. . . ? Pete, what are you doing with that gun?"

There was the sound of a horse coming down the hillside. I put my hands into my pockets deliberately. The boy let the gun-barrel drop. We both turned stiffly to watch Beth approach, letting her horse pick its way in the stilt-legged way they have of going downhill.

She was wearing a light, immaculate, wide-brimmed Stetson with a briaded leather cord, a white silk shirt open at the throat, and the kind of high-class, tailored denim pants—I won't insult them by calling them jeans—that are constructed by sombody aware that men and women are shaped differently in the rear. She'd never gone in for sloppy clothes much, I recalled, not even for doing the housework or digging in the garden. She was only a few years younger than I, never mind the exact figure, and she'd had three kids—my kids—but she looked like a slender girl on the back of the big horse.

I stepped forward to hold the animal as she reached us. She looked down at me from the saddle.

"Well, Matt," she murmured. "It seems like a long time, doesn't it?"

"You look like a movie cowgirl in that hat," I said. I jerked my head towards the kid with the carbine. "What's the reception committee for?"

She hesitated, and laughed quickly. "Let me introduce you. Peter Logan, my stepson. Mr. Matthew Helm." I waited, and she said, "Oh . . . why, we've been having trouble with rustlers, of all things! They'll drive in with a pickup or panel truck and butcher one of our steers and be off with the meat before anybody sees them. When Peter and I saw your truck from up above, we thought it best to investigate. . . . I didn't tell you to use a gun, Pete!" she said to the boy.

Peter Logan said quickly, "Dad said not to take any chances."

She said, "Well, if you'll lead my horse home, I'll drive back with Mr. Helm. . . ." About to dismount, she changed her mind. A gleam of mischief came into her eyes, and she gave me a glance, and spoke to Peter: "On second thought, suppose you lend Mr. Helm your horse. We'll cut back over the ridge and meet the boys while you bring his truck to the ranch."

Young Logan frowned. "Dad said for me not to let you ride anywhere alone."

"But I won't be alone," Beth said, laughing. "I'm sure Mr. Helm will take very good care of me."

I said, "Stick that carbine back in the scabbard, and I'll do my best to protect her from rustlers and outlaws."

The boy gave me a look that indicated he didn't think I was very funny. Then he turned on his heel, strode to the horse, rammed the Winchester into place, and came back leading the animal.

"We generally get on from the left, sir," he said, straight-faced. "It's just a local custom, but the horses are used to it."

"Sure," I said. "That's a four-speed shift in my truck. Reverse, in case you should need it, is to the left and back. Think you can manage?"

We looked at each other coldly. I was born in Minnesota, but I came west to horse country at an early age. He'd probably been driving old Chevy trucks before he was old enough to smoke.

"I'll manage," he said.

He turned and walked quickly to the pickup, kicked the starter, released the brake, and took off, throwing gravel from the rear wheels. I looked my new transportation over, and gave it a tentative pat on the nose. It didn't shy away or try to take my arm off, so I figured it was safe to climb aboard, and did so.

The stirrups were too short, and I'd forgotten about the Leica in my hip pocket, which didn't help me fit the saddle comfortably. Beth waited until I was mounted, wheeled her horse, and sent it up the hill with a rush. I gave my beast a couple of kicks and got it into motion, but she had to wait for me at the top.

"There's the ranch," she said, pointing.

It was in the valley beyond, a rambling collection of peeled-log buildings with enough large windows to qualify as rustic modern. It looked like quite a spread, as we say out West.

"Do you live there all year?" I asked.

"Oh, no," she said. "We move into town winters to be near the children's schools. And Larry has a little place in Mexico, too, where we go sometimes. . . . Follow me. We've got to head over this way to intercept the boy. Pete and I came straight down the mountain, but they'll be following the trail."

She took it fast. Her cross-country riding had improved since I'd seen her last. Undoubtedly this was why she'd decided to bring me to the ranch on horseback, to show off her new skill. Besides, she'd probably guessed I hadn't been on a horse for a year, and a man who's limping and saddle-sore is kind of at a disadvantage in delicate personal negotiations demanding an air of ease and dignity. I don't mean she was a malicious person or a calculating one. After all, we'd known each other for a long time. She was entitled to her little joke.

She led me around the side of the mountain, and pulled up at last in a wooded hollow, through the center of which ran a well-used trail. I checked my horse beside her; and she turned to face me, flushed and breathless from the ride. I thought she looked very attractive, but then, I'd been prejudiced enough on the subject to marry her, once.

"They'll be coming along soon," she said, "if they haven't already passed. I told them to head straight for home. There's a man with them, of course, but they ride very well now, both of them." She laughed. "We've even had Betsy on a pony. She's crazy to come riding with us, but she's a little small yet. She's barely three, you know."

"Yes," I said dryly, "I know. I happened to be present when she was born, if you'll remember. At least I was in the expectant papas' waiting room."

She flushed slightly. "Yes," she said. "Of course. . . . Well, we might as well get down and wait." She hesitated. "Besides . . . besides, there's something I have to tell you."

I said, "Yes, I got your note." When she did not speak at once, I went on idly, "I don't know as I have much faith in these rustlers of yours, Beth."

She said quickly, "Then you don't know much about modern ranching—"

"Oh, rustlers that slip in at night and make off with a beef now and then, sure. But not rustlers that cause your husband to give orders not to let you go riding in broad daylight without an armed escort. What's the trouble?"

She hesitated again. Her mount fidgeted, and she pulled it up sharply. "Let's get down, shall we?" she said. "I'm still not enough of a horsewoman to trust these animals completely."

"Sure."

I dismounted, and stepped forward to take her horse as she swung from the saddle. It was a funny damn experience, watching her. I mean, it had been a year, and I hadn't exactly spent it as a hermit. Whatever she'd meant to me once, I'd thought I was over it. But now, watching her drop lightly to the ground, I knew I should have stayed away.

She glanced at her watch, and looked up the trail. "I didn't realize we'd taken so much time. They're probably halfway to the ranch by now. Well, we can wait a few minutes longer and make sure."

Her voice was unnaturally level, but at least she had one. I wasn't quite sure how I'd sound if I tried to talk. I hadn't stayed away. I was here on a mountainside in Nevada, holding a couple of horses and watching her come forward—tallish, willowy, with big brown eyes and light brown hair under the big Stetson hat. She stopped in front of me.

I said, "Mrs. Logan."

My voice sounded about the way I'd expected it would. She glanced at me sharply. "Matt—"

I said, "It's a funny thing, Mrs. Logan, but you look just like a girl I used to know . . . a girl I used to know pretty well, as a matter of fact."

"Matt," she said. "Please! I should never—"

"No," I said. "You most certainly shouldn't. But you did."

I dropped the reins. If they were any kind of western horses, they ought to stand ground-hitched, and if they didn't, to hell with them. I reached out and took her by the shoulders, and she started to speak. She started to tell me not to touch her, but it would have sounded very corny, and she didn't say it. She started to tell me that she was happily married to a lovely guy named Logan, to whom she was deeply devoted, but she didn't say that, either.

It was all in her eyes, however, and I suppose I should have had the decency to leave her alone, but it had been a long year without her, and I didn't owe Logan a thing. All he'd ever done for me was marry my wife.

"Matt!" she whispered. "Please, no—"

I didn't really draw her towards me. At least, if I did, there wasn't any great resistance to overcome. Then she was in my arms, her face upturned, and her big hat fell off to hang down her back by its braided cord.

She was no longer trying to hold me off, quite the contrary. There was a disturbing kind of desperation in the way she clung to me. It wasn't really flattering. I couldn't kid myself she was thinking of me as a lover she'd missed; it was more that I was something solid and familiar and reassuring in a troubled world, and I suppose I should have been a gentleman and offered her an absorbent shoulder and an attentive ear instead of kissing her hard.

This changed the whole nature of the operation, as I had hoped it would. I'll be a rock of refuge if I have to, but only if I have to. Suddenly I wasn't any longer, and we'd known each other much too long and much too well for it to end with a kiss—and that was the moment our two boys picked to come charging down the hill, accompanied by a middle-aged cowboy who should have known better than to run a horse like that. Beth and I had barely time to jump apart and put respectable looks on our faces before they all raced into sight.

Chapter Four

LATER, Beth and I rode sedately down the trail while the boys and their escort ranged ahead. I noted that the man's horse, like the one I was riding, carried a lever-action .30-30 on the saddle.

My reunion with my sons had been undramatic. Matthew, age eight, had said 'Hi, Daddy,' and Warren, age six, had said 'Hi, Daddy,' and they'd both sat there uncomfortably on their ponies wondering if I'd brought them any presents from wherever I'd been, but too polite to ask. Then they'd ridden off, whooping. An extra daddy or two means very little, at that age, when you have a horse to ride.

Presently I heard a small sound from Beth. I glanced at her suspiciously. She kept her face averted as we rode along; then she looked at me quickly, and I saw that she was trying very hard to keep from laughing.

"Yeah, funny," I said, and grinned.

I mean, we'd been through it all before. It wasn't the first passionate moment in our lives that had been interrupted in this manner—in fact, I sometimes used to wonder how any parents ever managed to achieve more than one child. Somehow, after the first one, at the critical moment there's always a small voice outside the bedroom door telling you to come quick, the cat has just had kittens, the dog has just had pups, or there's a large brown bug in the bathtub. . . .

My truck was standing in the yard when we rode up. Beth glanced at it with a kind of nostalgia.

"I see the wheels haven't fallen off it yet," she said.

"Best damn car I ever had," I said. "I don't see your station wagon around."

"It needed a grease job, so Larry took it to town this

25

morning," she said. "He'll be back soon. I want you to meet him."

"Sure," I said.

"I really do," she said. "I think you'll like each other."

My friend, the young rifleman, came around a corner to take the horses. The boys, who'd reached the ranch well ahead of us, were all over him, telling him he had to come meet their real daddy. He was good with them, I saw, in that tolerant, mildly dictatorial way that, coming from someone they respect, someone three times their own age but still not too old to be approachable, goes down well with youngsters. He put them to work, giving them each a horse to lead away and unsaddle, and reminding them not to neglect their own mounts.

Beth said, "Peter, could you ask Clara to get the baby up and dress her? She's had a long enough nap, and I'm sure her father would like to see her."

"Yes, ma'am," young Logan said, and went off.

Beth watched him go. "He's a nice boy," she said. "I suppose it's hardly to be expected that he should be enthusiastic about me. A bomb killed his mother in London during the war. After a lot of knocking around here and there, Larry brought the boy to this country. There were only the two of them for years. Of course, Peter was away at school a good deal of the time, but still, there's a kind of special relationship between a widowed man and an only son. . . . And then I came along, with three children! Naturally he can't help considering us as rivals. It speaks a lot for his character and training that he can be as nice to us as he is." She shook her head, dismissing the subject. "Well, I'm going to take a shower. Come on and I'll show you to your room, first." She hesitated. "Matt."

"Yes."

"It was a mistake. Let's not repeat it."

"If you say so," I said politely.

She said, "It would be all wrong and . . . and kind of complicated and unpleasant, wouldn't it? I don't know what I was thinking of. I. . . ." She drew a long breath. "Anyway, here comes Larry."

A car that I recognized was coming up the road to the ranch. She walked quickly towards the front of the house to meet it. I saw her pause briefly as she realized that the driver was not alone.

I saw a funny, hard look that I didn't recognize come to her face. Then she was going forward again, but not as rapidly as before. I held back, since it seemed advisable to give her time to prepare her new husband for my presence. When I approached, she was talking to him at the side of the station wagon; but it wasn't Lawrence Logan who caught and held my attention first. It was the young girl who'd got out of the car on the other side, and the dog this girl had with her.

Of the two, the dog was slightly more spectacular. I'd seen red-haired girls before, but this was the first gray Afghan hound I'd met. It's not a breed with which I'm really familiar—not many people are—and the few specimens I'd encountered previously had all been brown or tan. This one was a silvery, bluish gray. Like all Afghans, it was short-haired along the back and long-haired down the legs so that, lean and bony, it looked rather like a greyhound with shaggy cowboy chaps on. It had a long, narrow, inbred head and big pleading brown eyes; and when I first saw it, it was protesting against something by standing erect on its hind legs, waving its woolly forepaws skyward, as tall as the girl on the other end of the leash.

She wasn't exactly inconspicuous herself, since her hair was that wonderful reddish-golden color that I doubt any woman ever grew naturally, but who cares? It was done up kind of casually about her head, with a loose swirl in back secured by a few pins that didn't look very trustworthy. She was quite young, not tall, but well developed or, as the saying goes, stacked. In other words, except for a trim little waist and neat small wrists and ankles, she wasn't skinny anywhere.

She was wearing sandals that would have looked swell on a Florida beach but seemed slightly impractical on a Nevada ranch; and emerald-green, skin-tight pants, the narrow kind that terminate about six inches above the

ankles. You could hardly call them slacks since they
didn't have any. Above them, she wore a kind of thin,
loose jacket adorned with a wild, Japanese-looking print,
predominantly the same bright shade of green as the
pants. It was quite a costume. It seemed a pity for her to
waste it on us mountain folks. In Bermuda, it would have
gone over big.

What with Beth and Logan to think about, and the ex-
otic dog putting on its standing-bear act, and the boys
coming racing from the corral to admire it, and the other
attributes of the girl to consider, I hope I may be excused
for not paying immediate attention to her face—besides,
it was partly turned away from me, as she tried to
calm her panicky, rearing pet. She got it back to earth,
but it wasn't happy, and it stood there trembling with its
long, snaky tail tucked between its legs—something I
never like to see in a dog, nor am I very fond of these
narow-headed animals, in any case. Selective breeding is
all very well, but you ought to leave room for a few
brains.

"Matt," Beth was saying now, coming towards me, "I
want you to meet my . . . my husband. Larry, this is Matt
Helm."

The moment was upon us, and it was no time to be
staring at stray young females or their unlikely-looking
dogs. Logan was standing in front of me. He was pretty
much as Mac had described him, a spare, sinewy man in
khakis, very English, with a bushy, sandy moustache
and sharp blue eyes under sandy brows and lashes. He
was older than I'd expected him to be, however:
somewhere in his forties. I should have been ready for
that after learning that he had a son over twenty. The
British don't go in for child marriages much.

He held out his hand. It wasn't a sign of friendship, or
even a gesture of peace; it was just a gentleman greet-
ing a guest in the proper manner, regardless of possible
personal differences.

"I have," he said, "heard quite a bit about you, Mr.
Helm."

"Yes," I said. "Probably you'd have preferred to hear less."

After a moment, he smiled. "Quite," he said.

We'd made contact, at least. It seemed as if we might get around to understanding each other, with a little effort on both sides. We studied each other briefly, standing there, and I knew what Mac had meant when he said this man looked as if he might be able to take care of himself. It wasn't a look, as much as a smell or an aura. I tried to tell myself I was imagining things, or that if I wasn't, it was just that at some time Logan had been in somebody's army and had fought somebody's war, like most men of his generation and mine. But there are lots of men who've worn uniforms and fought battles and got nothing much out of it but a few unpleasant memories and an allergy towards military discipline. He wasn't one of those.

He started to speak, but Beth grabbed his arm. "Is that animal safe?" she asked, pointing to the dog, now flat on the ground like a bearskin rug, its head between its paws, obviously suffering agonies of shyness, while the two boys scratched and petted and stroked it, and asked questions of its owner.

"Yes," I heard the girl say, "they can run pretty fast. In rough country, they can outrun a greyhound."

"Gee!"

Logan was laughing at Beth. "I don't know how safe the animal is, my dear," he said. "But I assure you the boys are perfectly safe. Afghans are quite gentle, and this one seems to be rather a shrinking violet, even for its breed."

Beth was still looking over there. Her face had again that strange hardness that I couldn't recall having seen before.

"Why did you bring her here?"

"It's a male dog, Elizabeth," Logan said. I gave him a quick look. He was absolutely deadpan, but he was kidding her just the same, in his quiet British way.

"I wasn't referring to the dog," she said sharply.

"Oh," he said, still deadpan. "Why, I met her on the

street. She asked about Peter. They used to be quite
good friends, you know. Childhood playmates and all
that. When I said he was home, she asked if she could
come out with me. I could hardly refuse. She's had a
rather rough time, you know, with both parents. She
used to consider us as her second family, somewhat
preferable to her own. I did not want to hurt her feelings, even if . . . Here comes Peter now, with his hair
combed, something parental authority has never been
able to accomplish. Let us go inside and leave the children to their play. Are you a martini or a bourbon man,
Mr. Helm?"

"Either one," I said. "It depends on the circumstances. For the long haul, bourbon, but for a quick jolt,
nothing beats a martini. I think tonight may be classed as
a martini night, Mr. Logan."

"Ah, yes," he said.

"If you'll excuse me," I said. "I'll join you in a minute."

He glanced towards the door, where a colored maid,
was just bringing Betsy out, scrubbed and shining in a
crisp little dress.

"We'll be in the living room," Logan said, taking
Beth's arm and moving tactfully away.

I gave him a glance. It occurred to me that if I didn't
watch myself I was going to start liking the guy. Then I
turned to greet my daughter who, it turned out, wouldn't
have known me from Santa Claus, except that Santa
has a beard. When I came into the high-ceilinged living
room, it was empty. Then Logan came in through a door
near the fireplace which apparently led into a study or
office with an outside door of its own. He was carrying a tall drink. He gestured towards a stemmed glass
awaiting me on the little bar in the corner. I took a quick
drink out of it.

He said, "It's always a bit of a shock when they don't
remember you, isn't it? I had the same experience during the war." He raised his glass. "Well, cheers, and all
that sort of thing."

"Cheers," I said. "I gave them a few presents, stuff

I picked up over in Europe recently. I hope you don't mind."

"Not at all."

"Where's Beth?" I asked.

He said, "I asked Elizabeth to withdraw temporarily. There is something I wish to say to you, Mr. Helm. I thought it would be easier for us to talk in her absence."

"Sure," I said. "Do we conduct the negotiations sitting or standing?"

He smiled quickly. "I say, I am making this sound terribly formal, am I not? Have a seat, by all means. I recommend that big chair by the window." He indicated the one, and started forward to take another, facing it. "Mr. Helm . . ."

I'd picked up my drink. As I turned from the bar, I brushed against it, and the camera in my hip pocket struck wood with a solid, quite audible thump. I reached back instinctively to check on its welfare. He was still speaking in his polite way; but at the sound, and my motion, his voice stopped and his hand moved, very fast, towards the lapels of the khaki bush jacket he was wearing.

It was a gesture that called for some violent response on my part. Fortunately, my encounter with the boy, earlier, had put a guard on my reflexes. I merely stood still and waited. His hand stopped. I drew a long, slow breath and continued reaching back without haste, drew the Leica from my pocket, and laid it on the bar.

"I thought I'd get some pictures of the kids before I left," I said.

His face was quite wooden. His hand rose to straighten the knot of his necktie. "Quite so," he said.

Then there was silence in the big room. I wanted to laugh, or to cry. I had him taped now. The practiced, instinctive gesture had told me everything I needed to know about him. That's the trouble with holsters. They give you away too badly, shoulder-holsters in particular.

Not that a shoulder-holster isn't a neat rig for carrying a heavy weapon outdoors in winter; it is. It puts the weight up where it belongs, supported by a substantial harness, instead of down on a narrow belt that tries to cut you in two. You don't have to open your coat much to get at it if you need it, and the gun doesn't freeze up in the coldest weather. A good spring shoulder rig is surprisingly comfortable, the gun is safe even if you stand on your head, it's protected from the elements, and it doesn't get in the way around camp the way a belt gun will. The fact that it's relatively slow needn't worry the outdoorsman, who's not apt, these days, to meet a grizzly on the trail without warning.

That's speaking of a big revolver carried by a hunter or trapper. When it comes to small, flat, inconspicuous automatics packed by competent-looking gentlemen with exaggerated British accents, you're speaking of a different matter entirely. I looked at him grimly. I knew him now. I knew what it was I'd smelled or sensed about him, that Mac hat noticed, too. It was the smell of smoke, of gunsmoke. It never quite blows away, as I had reason to know.

It was funny, I suppose. This was what Beth had married, after leaving me because she couldn't stand being married to a man of violence—this slightly superannuated soldier of fortune, one of the armpit-gun boys, for God's sake!

Chapter Five

NEITHER of us said anything. He came forward slowly and put his glass on the bar. He was a pro; he hadn't spilled a drop. Well, neither had I. He picked up the camera idly.

"Wetzlar, Germany," he read, and looked up. "Can't say I'm terribly fond of the Germans, but they do make fine optical equipment, what?"

"Right," I said.

There was a kind of sadness in his face. He was clearly wondering if he should try to explain himself to me and ask for my understanding, not knowing that he already had it. I understood him, all right. I'd retired from violence once myself, right after the war. I'd been a respectable, reasonably prosperous citizen, with a nice home and family, only something had happened and it hadn't worked out. Something was happening to him, or he wouldn't be carrying the gun again.

Oh, it would be the same gun, the one from his old, bold, smoky days. He would have kept it, we all do, telling ourselves it's just a memento now, a souvenir of a life we've left behind, an old retainer pensioned after years of faithful service. I'd had a gun in a locked drawer for close to fifteen years after the war; then one day I'd had to take it out again. I'd used it and lost it, and now I had a soulless, new, issue-.38 in my boot, and one day, no doubt, I'd try putting that away in a drawer with all the memories that would have attached themselves to it by that time—but I'd still put it away loaded and ready.

He would have put the key in the lock and opened the drawer and buckled on the leather gear and slipped the gun into place, doing it reluctantly, for some compelling reason I still didn't know about—but he might just possibly have felt the cold breath of an old ex-

citement touch him lightly in the moment he held the
weapon in his hand. I had. Of course, he was older. Maybe he had forgotten. Some men did, or said they did.

I understood him perfectly. I even sympathized with
him in a way. That didn't mean I was going to give him
any help, or that I wouldn't take away from him anything that wasn't nailed down—and I didn't have the feeling Beth was nailed down very tightly.

I said, "There was somthing you wanted to tell me."

"Ah, yes," he said. He took a sip from his glass,
looked into it briefly, and looked up again. "My wife
wrote you a letter," he said.

"Yes."

"Afterwards," he said, "not certain that it had been
the right thing to do, she told me, don't you know?"

"I see."

He hesitated, and spoke bluntly: "I do not need any
help in taking care of my family, Mr. Helm."

"Right," I said.

"I hate to seem inhospitable," he said, "but you don't
look like a chap who'll suffer greatly from one delayed
meal. You can buy a good dinner when you get back
to Reno. In the future, if you wish to see your children
at reasonable intervals—I'll make no objections to that,
of course—let me know and I'll arrange for them to meet
you away from here. Do I make myself clear?"

"Quite," I said.

He smiled. "It's an easy accent to mimic, isn't it? I do
it myself to a certain extent. It is part of the camouflage,
shall we say? I think you know what I mean. I intend to
maintain it, just as I intend to maintain the other aspects
of my life here, free from disturbance."

I said, "It's nice work if you can get it. I couldn't."

"I know," he said. "As I said earlier, I've heard much
about you and, shall we say, guessed more? I intend to
profit by your errors. You did make some, you know."

"Everyone does," I said.

"Perhaps," he said. "But one can try to make as
few as possible, don't you know? An error I don't intend to make is to let you stay here. It is too bad. From

what I've heard and seen, you're a man I might like. I wish we could go hunting together, for instance. It would be an interesting experience, at least. And of course it would be highly civilized of both of us. But in some cases, civilization can be overdone. Please don't think I like being rude. You are the first person who has ever been turned away from this house hungry. But at least you did get a drink." He smiled at me in a thin sort of way. It wasn't a very nice smile. It hinted that this man could be an ugly customer when he wanted to. "I'd settle for that, old chap," he murmured. "I really would."

When I got outside again, the sun was low above the mountains to the west. I hadn't bothered to bring an exposure meter—the light out there is fairly predictable —so I just made an estimate and set the camera accordingly. As I did so, the voice of young Peter Logan reached me from around the corner.

"If you were in Guadalajara, you should have stopped by Lake Chapala to see us."

"I didn't know you'd be there. Anyway, I didn't feel much like seeing people." After a little, the girl said, "Did I tell you I've got a new car? Kind of a consolation prize. I guess, but who's going to complain about a Mercedes 190SL? Real leather upholstery and fitted luggage, no less. Choice!"

The boy laughed. "What's with this choice?"

"Hadn't you heard? Nothing's cool any more. Everything's choice. Keep current, man!"

The dialogue made me feel older than the Sierras. I moved away from it, rounded up the kids, and posed them for a group picture in front of the house. Then I moved in for a few individuals, starting with the boys, since I didn't intend to spend much time on them. One snapshot of a little boy does about as well in your wallet as another. With a little girl, though, you want to make sure you get her looking pretty.

Betsy got restive, waiting, and ran off to play with the monkey-dog, as she called it—and it did look kind of like a great gray monkey, with its long tail and fur-framed face. It was lying peacefully beneath the hitching rack to which it had been tied. I figured the child was safe enough there, and turned back to the boys. The next thing I knew, Betsy was screaming and the dog was rearing wildly. Apparently she'd startled it out of a sound sleep, causing it to jump up and away. The leash, pulling tight, had knocked her over; and the animal, towering above her in panic, had frightened her further.

The dog was crying, too, fighting the choke collar and wailing like a lost soul. The girl in the bright green pants came running around the corner of the house. I started forward, putting the camera away, not hurrying too much. I hadn't been an acting papa for some time, but I could still tell the difference between a hurt child and one that was merely scared and indignant.

The girl snatched the leash loose and led the prancing dog off a little ways, trying to talk it in to a landing. It was all over her, still hoverng on its hind legs, but she didn't seem concerned about a little dust on her fancy costume. On the other hand she wasn't taking her weird pet's troubles too seriously, either.

I heard her laughing tolerantly at the animal's antics as I bent over Betsy; then somebody shoved me violently aside. Beth was there, snatching up the child and hugging her tightly, and swinging around to look at the girl.

"Get out of here!" Beth gasped. "Get out and take that ... that beast with you!"

The girl's laughter died. "But, Mrs. Logan, Sheik didn't mean—"

"Get out!" Beth cried. "We don't want you here, can't you understand? Not you or anybody else named Fredericks!"

It actually took me a little while, say a full second, to remember where I'd heard the name before.

Chapter Six

THEN I WAS back in Washington, in the basement room with the projector, and Smitty's voice was
saying: *Martell was seen in Reno recently, carrying a
gun for a racketeer named Fredericks*. It wasn't an un-
common name; it could have been a coincidence. I'd
worked for Mac much too long to believe it for an instant, but the meaning escaped me, for the moment.

Beth was still kneeling in front of me, hugging Betsy
and glaring at the Fredericks girl. I would have thought
she was being very unreasonable, if I hadn't remembered
the guns on the saddles and under Logan's armpit, and
her own evasive talk of cattle rustlers, for God's sake!
Obviously everyone here was under heavy pressure of
some kind.

"Get out!" Beth cried.

There was a little silence. The girl turned sharply
away. "Sheik, heel!" she commanded, and marched off
down the road with the big dog moving obediently beside her.

We watched them draw away. Beth raised her head
abruptly. "Peter, where are you going?"

The boy had started across the yard towards a rustic
carport, beneath which stood a racy-looking green Jaguar
two-seater, and one of those big four-wheel-drive Land
Rover station wagons they use for hunting in Africa—
apparently the master of the place still went in for
British machinery. Peter stopped and looked back de-
fiantly. It was time for me to take a hand, before this
developed into a serious family crisis.

"It's all right, Pete," I said, moving towards the truck.
"I was leaving, anyway. I'll see that she gets home."

The boy hesitated. Clearly he'd have liked to play the
role of rescuer himself. Logan's voice checked him, as he

was about to speak. "All right, Peter. Mr. Helm will take care of it."

"Yes, sir."

I opened the truck door, and looked back. Logan was at Beth's side, erect in his faded khakis and bush jacket. The gun didn't show at all. He looked like the great white hunter. Maybe he'd been that, too. I gave him a kind of salute and he answered it. As I got into the truck, I heard him speak to Beth.

"There was no need for a scene, my dear. The girl has nothing to do with—"

"How do you know?" she retorted. "She's his daughter, isn't she? He could have sent her to—"

I had to close the door before it became obvious that I was listening, so I lost the rest of it. I kicked the starter and drove away without further ceremony, pasing close by the boy as I made my turn in the yard. He glowered at me suspiciously. Obviously he had no faith in me as the champion of innocent womanhood. I didn't blame him a bit. I didn't have much faith in me, in that respect, myself.

I caught up with her after about a quarter of a mile, and slowed down to appreciate the sight briefly, before I pulled alongside. I never saw two more intriguing rear ends in my life: the big Afghan with its furry legs and long wispy tail, and the compact, wonderfully well-shaped girl in her tight green pants. She was striding right along, despite her inadequate sandals, with the sun bright on her red-gold hair, which was starting to come down in places. It always does, when they wear it like that, and are that young. Maturity seems to be necessary for a woman to wear her hair up and keep it there.

The dog was following effortlessly at her side, and in motion it was a different animal from the canine clown we'd seen at the ranch. It didn't move like any dog I'd ever seen, but more like a thoroughbred horse. Overbred and shy and temperamental it might be, and probably stupid as well, but it was a hell of a beautiful thing, in motion.

Neither of them looked around as I drove up. The dog

did start to lunge aside, frightened, but she spoke to it sharply and it settled back into place beside her. They both kept walking stubbornly down the endless mountain road, heads up, faces forward.

I leaned out of the cab window. "The dog can probably make it," I said, "but I have my doubts about you, in those shoes."

She walked a little farther. Abruptly she stopped and wheeled to face me. There were little shiny tear-tracks down her cheeks, I was startled to see. I hadn't judged her to be a crying girl. She didn't speak at once. She seemed to be sizing me up. I got a leisurely look at her for the first time. She had a wide mouth, a kind of pug nose that wasn't unattractive, and disturbing sea-green eyes that didn't belong in that half-pretty, half-cute kid's face. In a Moslem country, robed and veiled, she'd have had grown men doing flips, with those eyes.

After a moment, she lifted her hands and tucked her hair up quickly all around, and glanced at the dog sitting nicely beside her, watching her.

"I'd better put him in back," she said.

"If he makes a mess on my bedding," I said, "you clean it up."

"He's very good," she said stiffly. Abruptly, she bent down and put her arms around the dog's neck, hiding her face. I heard a sound that might have been a sob. I set the brake and got out and opened up the rear of the truck's canopy, and dropped the tailgate. Presently she led the dog up to me, straight-faced now, and looked inside. "What's in that box?" she asked.

"A few groceries."

"You'd better take the bread and bacon up front," she said. "That's asking a little too much of him."

"Sure," I said.

It took the two of us to load him aboard. He panicked again, and we had to pick him up bodily and stuff him inside, about seventy pounds of him, mostly legs. I made sure the side windows of the canopy were open to give him air, and closed up the rear.

"That," I said, as we got into the cab, "is quite a dog
you've got there." I started the truck.

She gave me a sideways glance. "If you'd been brought
up in kennels for the best part of your life, you'd be a little shy with humans, too. He'd never been inside a house
when I got him, or outside a fence. He's really coming
along very well." She made a little sniffing sound. "You
don't happen to have a tissue around, do you? I seem to
be allergic to the dust or something."

"Yeh," I said, watching the road. "It gets people. Try
the glove compartment."

She blew her nose, and went on talking briskly. "He's
really a wonderful dog. Very gentle. Very clean. I hardly
had to do a thing to housebreak him. And he hardly ever
barks and disturbs people." After a little, she said, "You
know, it's sort of a challenge, taking a dog like that, almost a wild thing, and teaching it to . . . to trust you. I
mean, I had a little Shepherd bitch that I was very fond
of—I almost died when she was hit by a car—but it
wasn't the same thing. She was just born to serve humanity, if you know what I mean. She was positively frantic
to learn things so she could do them for you. Sheik,
well, he just doesn't give a damn for humanity, or thinks
he doesn't. At first, he'd only come to me for food. It
was like having a half-tame deer around the place. . . .
Well, when you get a dog like that to wag his tail for
you just once, because he's finally decided it's safe to
like you a little, you've accomplished something. Oh, he's
still got a long way to go, but we're gaining."

I didn't say anything. I just drove the truck and let
her talk herself out. She took another tissue from the
glove compartment and blew her nose again.

"He was just what I needed," she said. "Kind of
therapy, if you know what I mean. You see, I was living
in New York and doing a little work at Columbia after
getting myself kicked out of—well, never mind that. Anyway, I got mixed up with a man, a married guy, and it
wound up in kind of a mess all around, if you know
what I mean. And then my other dog got run over, and I
was about ready to jump off one of the bridges, it was

just a matter of deciding which one, they've got plenty to choose from in that damn town, and then I was just driving around on Long Island and I happened to see this kennel along the road. I went in and told them to trot out the wildest, meanest, most difficult dog they had, one that nobody else wanted. I didn't even know what kind of dogs they raised, or care. They brought out Sheik. He wasn't mean—he's never even thought of touching me with his teeth—but he certainly was spooky and difficult. You should have seen him take off when we first snapped a leash on him. Honest, I thought we'd have to go after him with a helicopter and butterfly net. . . . Your name is Helm, isn't it?" she said abruptly.

"Yes."

"You used to be married to Pete's stepmother. He told me."

"That's right."

"You lucky man," she said. "You lucky, lucky man." She blew her nose again.

I said, "If you run out of tissues, there's another box up behind the seat."

She said, "I'm not really the weepy type, normally. Only . . . well, Sheik's all right, but his vocabulary's kind of limited, if you know what I mean. It was nice to talk to human beings for a change. I've been away so much I don't have any friends here, except the kind you pick up in bars and play the slot machines with."

I glanced at her, sitting there. "That's not the only thing they want to play, I'll bet."

She said, "Are you kidding? None of those creeps dares even look at me hard. They're all so scared of Dad they wouldn't be seen within a block of my place for fear he might misinterpret . . ." Her voice, which had hardened perceptibly, stopped. She turned to look at me. "My dad is Big Sal Fredericks. The racketeer, I guess you'd call him. But you know all about that, don't you?"

"What do you mean?"

"I saw your face, when you heard my name. It meant something to you, didn't it? What did it mean?"

I moved my shoulders. "Very little, Miss Fredericks. I'd heard the name before, that's all."

She laughed shortly. "Don't be so damn cautious, you're not the type. . . . Dad thinks I still believe he's in the hotel business. At least he'd like me to pretend I believe that." She laughed again. "The hotel business! Choice, isn't it? I've known better since I was nine. . . . All those damn schools, always at the other end of the country, somewhere, and always they'd find out and start whispering. . . . Pete Logan had it the same, of course, except that it was a little easier for him. His dad wasn't so well known, just Big Sal's bodyguard and right-hand man. And then, suddenly, Duke Logan wasn't there any more, just a tough character with a broken nose; and I wasn't supposed to go out to the Logan ranch, or visit the place in Mexico winters like I used to; and then they made up and I could go there again, but the Duke never came back to work for Dad, and he'd never tell me the reason. And now his wife kicks me off the place, calling down curses on the name of Fredericks. Corny! But if your name happened to *be* Fredericks, you'd want to know why, wouldn't you?" She drew a long, ragged breath. "I don't mean just words I've heard all my life, like racketeer and gangster. I mean *exactly* why."

Chapter Seven

WE REACHED town well after dark. It's a gaudy place at night, Reno, self-proclaimed the biggest little city in the world, and we drove through it in silence. Following her directions, I turned into a neat residential area where we stopped in front of a little blue California-type house, probably two bedrooms, bath, living-dining room, and a small, shiny efficient kitchen. Hardwood floors and plenty of closet space would be included in the price, but no character or individuality whatever.

"Just pull up in the drive," she said, and I stopped behind a white sports car parked on the gravel. She seemed to feel that the house required explanation, and said, "It's kind of a big place for just one person, but it wouldn't have been fair to Sheik to try keeping him in an apartment. The neighbors are going crazy trying to figure me out, living here alone." Her voice was dry. "When they do, they'll probably get up a petition to have my lease canceled. Well, thanks for the lift."

I said, "I'll give you a hand with that junior-grade horse."

It took the two of us, again, to get him unloaded. He wouldn't be pulled; I finally had to get in with him and scare him out into her arms. I had my doubts about this maneuver—the beast had jaws and teeth, remember—but apparently I frightened him a lot more than he frightened me. He just cowered against the side of the truck bed until I got behind him; then he made a flying leap outwards. She was ready for him, but seventy pounds of dog was too much for her and she went down in the gravel. She rolled over acrobatically and managed to grab the end of the leash she'd dropped in the fall.

"Now, Sheik," she said mildly, picking herself up. "Well, thanks again," she said to me. "I hope the true

43

confessions didn't bore you stiff. Catharsis, those head-shrinker characters call it, don't they?"

"Something like that."

"Do you want to come in? I've got liquor and ice, and I think there's some hamburger left."

She was brushing herself off in the rear as she spoke. Her voice was as casual as it could possibly be, but her disturbing eyes were very steady on my face. I was being tested. This was where I showed whether I was really a nice guy, or just another middle-aged jerk with an eye for youth and beauty.

"It sounds intriguing," I said, and her eyes narrowed slightly, and I went on, "but I'll have to take a rain-check. I got about twelve hours behind on my sleep, driving across the desert last night."

"Where are you staying?"

"The Riverside Motel," I said.

She hesitated, and asked abruptly, "Do you like hunting?"

"Sure," I said, "but there's no season open that I know of. Besides, I'd have to get an out-of-state license, and they run pretty steep."

She reached down and stroked the dog's lean head. "He doesn't need a license, and there's no closed season on jack rabbits," she said. "At least, no game warden has arrested me yet. It's . . . kind of interesting to watch. I thought I might go out tomorrow. Would you like to come along?"

"Sure," I said. "Just don't make it too early."

"We could take your truck and save me beating up my little imported jewel, here, on those roads. I'll call you."

She turned quickly and marched into the house with the big dog. The door closed and the lights went on. I frowned thoughtfully. One thing you learn, in this business, is not to take for granted you're just naturally the kind of guy pretty young girls want to do things with, even if it's only watching a dog chase a rabbit.

I gave her parked car another glance as I turned away. It was the small, ladylike Mercedes sports, not the big hot one. Even so, it was quite a car, a good six thousand dollars' worth with extras. I got into my old pickup—worth about two hundred bucks on a trade-in, if the salesman was hungry—and drove back to the motel, and parked in front of the end unit, which was mine.

I got out, and gave the door a careful look as I approached it. Certain indications showed that nobody'd been through it since I had. I laughed at myself for taking such precautions. After all, I was on vacation. I put the key in the lock, and something moved in the ornate shrubbery to my right. A voice spoke in a kind of choked whisper.

"Eric . . ."

I had my hand on the little knife in my pocket. It was made in Solingen, Germany, and I liberated it during the war, the previous owner having no further use for it. It's not much larger than an ordinary pocket knife, but it's big enough. The blade locks in the open position, so you don't have to worry about its folding over and cutting off your fingers if you happen to strike bone as you go in. But the voice had used my code name. I worried the key left-handed, as if the lock were giving me trouble.

"Name yourself," I said without turning my head.

"Paul."

I waited. He was supposed to say a certain identifying phrase now, and I was supposed to answer with another phrase. Instead, he made a little moaning sound.

"For God's sake, man! Give me a hand, quick. I . . . I've been waiting. . . . I'm hurt. . . ." There was what you might call an expiring sigh.

I didn't say anything. I've been kidded before, by real good actors. I took the knife out and opened it, muffling the click against my body. Anybody could have got our code names, any time. Unlike the recognition signals, they were never changed. My humanitarian instincts had atrophied long ago. I wasn't diving blindly into any bushes to give first aid to a disembodied, suffering, unidentified voice.

Nobody spoke and nothing happened. I'd stood there fiddling with the lock long enough. I turned the key and went inside fast. As the untouched door had indicated, nobody was waiting for me there. Having made sure of that, I turned on the light, folded the knife and put it away, and got the .38 revolver out of my boot and checked it over. It's a sawed-off, stripped-down, aluminum-framed little monster with too little weight to soak up the recoil of the big cartridges, particularly in rapid fire, but at the moment I was happy to have it.

I noted the time on my watch: seven minutes past eight. Fifteen minutes ought to do it, I figured: long enough to let them know I wasn't going to fall for the gag, if it was a gag, long enough for them to pull out and think it over, but not long enough for them to set up any fancy alternatives. And if my fellow-operative, the young guy Mac didn't think was going to work out for us, Paul, was really out there, hurt . . . well, since he hadn't been able to come up with the proper signals, he'd just have to sweat it out as long as it took me to do this right.

We're not a little band of brothers, if you know what I mean. It's a point of pride with us that nobody's ever blown a mission because he hung around sentimentally to care for a wounded pal. The standing orders are very strict on this point. Not that I had a mission yet, but it seemed likely I'd have one soon, one way or another, and I intended to stay alive to execute it.

I'd been given a bunch of good-will stuff when I checked into the place. Now I took it over to the bed and lay down to read it with the gun handy. There was a list of other motels in this particular chain, which seemed to cover most of the states west of the Mississippi. There was a list of eating places in town, and a sketchy map of the town, and a small instruction book designed to make the various forms of gambling more comprehensible and attractive to the untutored tourist.

There was also a courtesy copy of a daily paper. I made myself read it without checking my watch too often. The international situation was going to hell in a basket, as usual. The local politics were as mysterious as they always are in a place where you know nothing and nobody. A house had been broken into. A guy had been robbed on the street. A technician at a nearby government laboratory—I remembered all those installations I'd passed in the dark—had died after suffering massive radioactive contamination when something went bang that wasn't supposed to.

A woman and a child had been killed in a head-on collision with a big truck. The truck-driver had survived with minor injuries. They usually do, which is one reason why I'm still driving my high and tough and massive old vehicle instead of getting something low and glamorous. . . .

I got up and looked at the door. There had been no sound for fifteen minutes. Well, if they wanted me, and were willing to make enough noise, they'd get me, now or an hour from now. I walked out with the gun in my hand. It was warmer outside than in the air-conditioned motel room. Nothing happened. I got into the truck and drove away. Nobody followed.

When I'd confirmed this, I stopped at a pay telephone booth and called Washington collect, calling the emergency number. The girl who came on at once wanted to give me Mac, but I said she could keep him.

"Has Paul reported recently? Is he overdue?" I asked.

"He has no fixed schedule. His last report was the day before yesterday."

"I may need a doctor who'll keep his mouth shut," I said. "Have we got one locally?"

"Just a minute." I heard papers rustle, two thousand and some miles away. "Dr. Ditsinger. We've never used him, but other agencies have, and found him satisfactory. Do you want him alerted?"

"Please."

She told me the address. "Give us a few minutes to get in touch with him."

"It's not definite," I said. "Check back with him in the morning. If he's had no business, tell him to forget it. If he's got a customer, tell the man upstairs that age will take the reins from the faltering hands of youth. As if he didn't know it."

"I'm sorry. I didn't get that, sir. Please repeat."

"Skip it, doll. Just report that if young Paul should be

out of commission, which seems to be a possibility, I'll
take over. But in that case I want somebody else to get
out here fast and stand by. No contact unless I call,
however. I've got enough people crawling through the
shrubbery already; the management might squawk. Oh,
one question."

"Yes, sir?"

"Has Paul made definite identification of his subject?"

The papers rustled again. "Yes, sir. In his last report.
Quote: 'Subject Martell definitely established to be man
calling himself Fenn currently employed by Salvatore
Frederici, alias Sally Fredericks or Big Sal Fredericks, re-
puted to be head of narcotics trade locally, as well as—' "

"Narcotics, eh?" I interrupted. "The stuff seems to
keep cropping up. Rizzi was also in that racket. I wonder
what Martell. . . . Never mind. If Paul had made identification, why didn't he take action? What are we saving
this guy for, somebody's birthday or the anniversary of
the Russian Revolution?"

"I have the agent's instructions here." More papers
rustled. "No action to be taken until subject's mission is
fully understood."

You could see that Mac might be curious about why a
top agent like Martell would play at being a cheap hood
for seven years, but his curiosity could get expensive in
human lives. Maybe it already had.

I said, "All right. Say I'll call back when I have something to report."

"Yes, sir."

She had a nice voice, but it wasn't any time to be
thinking about nice voices or the girls who went with
them. I hung up and drove back to the motel. I could
have saved myself the trouble of arranging for a doctor.
He was lying in the bushes, all right, but there was nothing any doctor could do for him. He'd been beaten to
death, or as close to it as made no difference in the
long run. Even in the dark, it wasn't a very pleasant
sight. It never is.

I squatted beside the body for a little while. As far as
I could make out, he'd been a blond boy in his

twenties, and he could have been one of those I'd trained with the previous year. They hadn't been assigned code names yet, when I left. I thought I recognized him, but somebody had done a very thorough job, and it was hard to be sure. Well, it didn't make much difference now.

I waited until the premises were clear of people for a moment, carried him out of there, and loaded him into the truck. I took him to Dr. Ditsinger, anyway. I acted surprised and terribly shocked when I was informed that my friend was dead. Controlling myself with a manly effort, I told Ditsinger to call Washington for further instructions, and got the hell out of there with my grief.

Chapter Eight

DRIVING BACK, I slowed as I crossed the bridge over the Truckee River. There wasn't much doubt about how Paul had reached the motel: his clothes had been soaking wet. They must have tossed him into the river somewhere upstream. How he'd managed to make it from there, in his condition—crawling, wading, swimming where the water was deep enough—only God or a dying man could tell you.

Why he'd done it was another interesting question. It was possible, of course, that he'd been bringing me information of tremendous importance. It was just as possible that he'd just been looking for somebody to hold his hand.

I shivered slightly, and drove on, and turned into the motel area, and parked where I had before. I went inside and poured myself a drink from the plastic flask I carry in my suitcase. I kept hearing a voice saying, *For God's sake . . . I'm hurt. . . .* Well, that was all right. I'd heard voices before. I could live with one more. But I drank the whiskey anyway. Then I got out of my clothes and went into the bathroom to take a shower. Just as I was about to turn on the water, the doorbell rang.

I sighed. I went to the closet and got my dressing gown. I dropped the gun into the pocket, after belting the garment about me. Then I went to the door and yanked it open. So maybe they'd traced Paul here somehow and now it was my turn. I was tired of being careful. I'd been careful enough for one night. To hell with them. I'd get at least one before they burned me down, I would.

The traumatic shock of seeing the door fly open before his eyes sent the Afghan hound into a tizzy; he

50

lunged away and almost yanked the Fredericks girl over backwards. He was really a specimen.

"Oh, Sheik!" she said impatiently, and to me: "Just a minute while I tie him."

I was having a little trouble getting used to the idea that I didn't have to sell my life dearly, at least not yet.

"What he needs," I said sourly, "is a mooring mast, like a dirigible."

"Mister," she said, "I can make cracks like that, but don't you go criticizing other people's dogs. Hell, you can't even keep a wife." She straightened up to look at me. "Well, aren't you going to ask me in?"

"Do I have to?"

She made a face at me, and stepped inside. I followed her, and pulled the door closed behind us. She was no longer wearing the green beach costume, if that was what it was. Now she was done up in a simple white dress that could have cost ten bucks or a hundred, probably the latter, and white kid pumps with high, slim heels. Her hair was smooth and shining about her head, every pin doing its assigned duty. She even had little white gloves on, very formal for Reno.

I can itemize the assets of a girl in pants without becoming emotionally involved in any way. I have to see her in a dress before I can add up the column and become personally involved in the total. This was a good dress for the purpose, straight, smart, and sleeveless, with a square neck. The material was some textured cotton stuff —piqué is the word that comes back from my rare forays into fashion photography. She wasn't wearing any jewelry. There weren't any distractions tonight in the way of fancy style, color, or decoration. You could concentrate on the girl, and any man would.

I said, "Okay, so you're beautiful. Now can I go take my shower?"

She said, "You're a liar. I'm not beautiful and I never will be. I'm just sexy as hell."

I said, "You're drunk as hell, too."

She shook her head. She was pulling off her gloves, making herself at home. She said, "No, I'm not drunk. I

just had one when I got home—you did, too, by the looks
of that flask—and then I started thinking about that damn
hamburger and it made me kind of sick. And then I
started thinking about going out to eat alone, and that
made me kind of sick, too. So here I am. Make yourself
respectable. You're taking me to dinner."

I studied her for a moment. If she was acting, she was
very, very good.

I said, "You forgot a word, didn't you?"

She frowned briefly. "What do you mean?"

"It begins," I said, "with a 'P'."

She looked at me. Something happened in those odd,
green eyes. She licked her lips. "Please?" Then she said
breathlessly, "Please! I'm going nuts in that damn big
house with nothing but a damn dog to talk to. I'll pay
for—"

"Cut," I said. "End of take, as they say in Hollywood.
Sit down and smoke something somewhere, if you can
find it. I'll be with you in a minute."

I got a pair of slacks and a jacket out of the closet, a
shirt from my suitcase, gathered up the necessary acces-
sories, and went into the bathroom.

"Help yourself, if you want a drink," I called, hanging
up my dressing gown. "You'll have to get ice from the
machine outside."

Her voice came from directly behind me. "My God,
what happened to you?"

I was just pulling on my shorts. I managed to control
the outraged-modesty reaction to the point where I
merely finished what I was doing and turned to look at
her. She was standing in the opening, one hand on the
bathroom door, which she had pushed back silently.

"Happened?" I asked. "What do you mean?" She gestured towards various marks on the still exposed por-
tions of my anatomy. I said, "Oh, those. I was blown up
in a jeep during the war and had to have various hunks
of old iron taken out of me."

"Old iron?" she said. "Old lead, you mean! I know
bullet-scars when I see them. Duke Logan has a couple
that show when he takes off his shirt."

"Good for old Duke."

"Who are you, Helm?" she whispered. "What are you doing here? What do you want?"

I went up to her, and put my hand out, and pushed her back a step. "I want you to get the hell out of here so I can get dressed," I said, and then I knew I had made a serious mistake.

It had been a long day. I was in a susceptible mood, I guess, after that incident with Beth in the mountains. I was wound up with various emotions and tensions that needed an outlet. I shouldn't have got that close to the kid. I shouldn't have touched her.

Everything had changed suddenly, the way it does. We both knew it. She stood quite still in the doorway, looking up at me.

"Are you sure that's what you want?" she murmured, and now her green eyes were laughing at me as I stood there in my shorts with, no doubt, naked desire in my eyes.

I said, "Honey, if you don't look out, you're going to get that nice dress all mussed."

"It doesn't muss very easily," she said calmly. "That's why I wore it here. But if it worries you, take it off."

She was smiling as she turned slowly around to let me unzip and undress her, if I dared. It was a kid's game and I was damned if I was going to play it with her. I just picked her up and carried her over to the nearest bed and dumped her upon it so hard that she bounced. She looked up at me indignantly from beneath the bright hair that had suddenly tumbled into her face.

I said, "If you were just playing, say so. I'm too old to play games with sex."

She licked her lips childishly. Then she smiled. "Nobody's that old," she murmured.

She was right, of course.

Chapter Nine

IT WAS A big dining room high up in some Reno hotel, but you couldn't really tell by looking. You only knew it because you'd used an elevator to get there.

In Europe, they'd have had a little roof garden where you could sip your cocktail, apéritif, or aquavit outdoors, and look at the lights of the town, and the mountains beyond, while you conversed intelligently about matters that had nothing to do with love—at least the words didn't. Then you'd go inside to a nice big table with a white tablecloth and plenty of room around it and be served an exquisite dinner by waiters who took pride in their work. . . . I don't want to sound subversive or unpatriotic. They do some things worse over there and some things better. Eating is one of the things they do very well.

This was a table about the size of one of the new small tires on one of the new small cars. There were, roughly speaking, a million of these tables crammed into the room —a slight exaggeration, but that was the general effect. There wasn't space enough left for the waiters to maneuver conveniently. They had to ooze through the cracks by a process of osmosis. Maybe this was what had ruined their dispositions, or maybe they'd never had any to start with.

At the end of the room was a stage, and on the stage, assisted by an orchestra of sorts, a man was singing. Well, let's call him a man, just for purposes of reference, and I suppose it went under the name of singing. I looked at the girl on the other side of the table. She was the right age, or close enough to it, to explain the phenomenon to me.

54

"Does he send you?" I asked. "Does he arouse anything in you?"

"Yes, sure, my maternal instinct," she said. "I've got a practically irresistible yearning to go up there and change his diapers and see if he'll stop crying."

Her resilience was fantastic. Nobody looking at her would have dreamed that less than half an hour ago she'd been lying on a rumpled bed, flushed and breathless, with her nice dress bunched immodestly about her waist and her bright hair tumbled untidily over the pillow. Now she looked cool and crisp and immaculate again, and even kind of innocent, as if a sinful thought had never crossed her mind—at least not since she'd put those fine clothes on. Only her eyes had changed, a little, and maybe that was just my imagination. You like to think it's made some difference to the girl.

She reached out abruptly and touched my arm with a white-gloved hand. "Just one thing," she said. "Don't say anything about Lolita. Promise."

"I wasn't going to—"

"That other guy, the one in New York, I was his lousy Lolita all the lousy time. I thought it was cute until I read the book. What a pill! Anyway, I'm no teen-age kid. Just because he was a few years older. . . . Just because you are, don't start thinking. . . . If you say one damn thing about Lolita, I'll get up and walk out."

I glanced at the loose-lipped, wailing character on the stage and said, "It might not be half a bad idea, if I get to go with you."

"Well, I just wanted to tell you. No Lolita."

"In that case," I said, "you'd better tell me your name, hadn't you?"

She looked a little startled. "Don't you know?"

"Fredericks I know. Not what goes before."

"It's Moira. Isn't that corny?"

"Not particularly," I said. "Mine's Matt."

"I know," she said. She looked around, as if seeing her surroundings for the first time. "Don't you like it here?" she asked. "We can go someplace else if you don't like it."

She'd recommended the place. I said, "I'm just spoiled, I guess. In Europe you get less noise and more atmosphere."

"It is kind of crowded," she admitted, "but the food's supposed to be good." Her green eyes touched me lightly. "What were you doing in Europe, Matt?"

"Business," I said.

"What kind of business?"

I didn't answer at once. I didn't particularly want to lie to her; besides, nobody'd supplied me with a real cover for this job, and when you start making it up as you go along, you're apt to talk yourself into a corner.

Her hand was still on my arm. "You're a government man, aren't you?" she murmured, watching me closely.

"A G-man?" I said. "Now, do I look like one of Mr. Hoover's fine, upstanding, clean-cut young men? Why those fellows are selected for character and integrity. If I'd been one of them, you'd never have seduced me in a million years. I'd have been a rock, I tell you: solid, immovable, granite."

She smiled at me across the table. "All right, Matt, I'll try not to ask questions. Anyway, I wasn't thinking of the FBI. I had in mind—" She hesitated, and looked down at her glass, containing something that was supposed to be a martini—well, there probably was some gin in it, somewhere, judging by my own specimen. I won't answer for the vermouth. She looked up quickly. "I had in mind . . . a certain branch of the Treasury Department."

I said, "I've never investigated an income tax in my life."

She frowned slightly, withdrawing her hand. "You're ducking awfully hard, baby."

"You're pushing hard. Why can't I just be Mrs. Logan's cast-off husband?"

"With those scars? And the way you looked when you heard the name Fredericks, and—" She looked down. "You can't blame me for wanting to know. As a matter of fact—"

"What?" I said when she hesitated.

"As a matter of fact, I didn't come to your motel *just*

because I was lonely. I was. . . . well, kind of curious, too."

Her face was pink. I grinned. "You were going to play Mata Hari, is that it?"

She said, with some stiffness in her voice, "I haven't done too badly, baby. You're her ex-husband, all right, I don't suppose there's any doubt about that. But you're something else, too. Something—" She hesitated.

"Something what?"

"Something kind of special, in a gruesome sort of way." She didn't smile. "I've met a lot of them, you know; I've spent my whole life, it seems, falling over snoopers of one kind or another trying to get something on Dad. Half of them had their hands out wanting to be bought off—ninety per cent is closer, I guess—and the rest were so sincere they made you sick, saving suffering humanity, for God's sake. Those I can spot a mile off, both kinds. But I don't dig you, baby. You're not hungry and you're not particularly sincere. It makes me wonder just what you're after."

I hesitated, and asked, "How much do you care for your old man, Moira?"

"I hate his guts," she said readily enough. "He put my mother away in an . . . in a home, I guess you'd call it. Some home! She could probably have been cured, lots of alcoholics are, but he couldn't take the trouble. I guess he just didn't want her around drinking tomato juice at his parties and reminding people that Sal Fredericks' wife had been a helpless lush; anyway, she wasn't very pretty any more, and he likes his women decorative. So he had her put away, in a nice friendly place where she could drink herself to death without disturbing anybody. She hasn't quite made it yet, but she's working on it. . . ." Her eyes were intent on my face. "That's the answer to your question. But if you're asking what I think you're asking. . . . Don't get any wrong ideas, Matt. I didn't pick him and he didn't pick me, but there are certain things you can't do a damn thing about. He's my pop and I'm stuck with him, if you know what I mean."

"I know," I said. "I know what you mean."

"It's corny," she said. "I know, these days if your best friend turns out to be a Red or a crook or something, you're supposed to turn him in right now; it's your duty to society and to hell with friendship and personal loyalty and all that crap—people used to die for it, but nowadays it's crap. And as for family ties, I went to college, I learned all about it. I know it's perfectly all right if Junior takes an axe to ma and pa. He's just getting rid of his repressions, the dear little thing. But the plain lousy fact, Matt, is that I'm not one of those complex types, and I'm just a real lousy citizen; I don't give a damn about my duty to society. I'm a dumb and simple country girl, and my old man is my old man. Even if he's a sonofabitch, he's my sonofabitch." She drew a long breath. "What I'm trying to say is—"

I said, "It's all right, kid. I know what you're trying to say. Even if the situation should arise, I won't ask you for help. And I'm really not very interested in your old man. Honest Injun."

She ignored this. "What I'm trying to say is, maybe you're a swell guy and maybe you're saving the country, but I'm not going to be a stool pigeon or a judas goat for anybody."

"I read you loud and clear," I said. "Drink your martini; you'll never find another like it, I hope."

She hesitated. After a moment, she said, "Matt."

"Yes?"

"I was coming back from Mexico a couple of weeks ago. They stopped me at the border. You know, usually they don't pay much attention to you, coming out of Juarez. You tell them you haven't bought much of anything except some cheap liquor, and they send you over to pay that lousy hold-up tax to the state of Texas, and that's it. But this time they gave me the works. They practically took the car apart. I thought they were even going to get a matron or something and make me strip, but I guess whatever they were looking for was bigger than that. When Dad heard about it, he almost blew his safety circuits."

"So?"

She looked at me steadily and said, "Damn you! It's dope, isn't it?"

There was a little pause. The waiter picked that moment to come up and stick his elbow in my face so he could put some food in front of her. Then he stuck his elbow in her face so he could put some food in front of me. He went away, proud that he'd remembered to serve us in the right order.

"Isn't it?" she said. "He's tried every other lousy racket; he was bound to get to it sooner or later. It's dope, and they're expecting him to receive a . . . a shipment, perhaps, and they thought maybe I was running it across the border for him?" She waited a little. I didn't say anything. She said, "Well?"

I said, "You're doing the guessing. Don't expect any help from me."

She sighed. "No. Of course not. But I think I'm right. That would explain why Duke Logan left him. The Duke always said he'd run guns to anybody who'd pay—he'd done it, too—but he drew the line at trafficking in dope and women."

"Good for old Duke," I said.

"Don't sound so cynical."

I said, "These guys who keep drawing lines never impress me very much. I know a dozen fishermen who'll let a trout fight its heart out against a nylon leader, but who are real proud of themselves because they've never shot anything in their lives. And then there's a man I know who'll shoot any bird that flies—ducks, geese, quail, doves, you name it—but he feels quite moral because he's never killed a big animal like a deer or an elk. And I even know a deer hunter who gets his buck every fall but who'd never dream of going to Africa and murdering a great big elephant just for sport, he thinks that's terrible. They've all got something they won't do, and it makes them feel swell."

She studied my face for a moment. "And you?" she murmured. "What won't you do, Matt?"

"Nothing," I said. "I draw no lines, kid."

She said, "We were talking about dope—"

"You were talking about dope."

"It's a lousy business, isn't it?"

I moved my shoulders. "I never could get very excited about saving people from themselves, but some folks seem to."

She said, "You're a funny man. You ought to be giving me a lecture on the evils of this horrible trade, showing me where my duty lies."

"I should worry about your duty," I said. "I've got trouble enough with my own."

"Yes," she said. "I just wish I knew what the hell it was." After a moment, she said, "There's something that worries me. I'm going to tell you about it. Probably I shouldn't, but I'm going to anyway."

"Think it over first," I said.

She laughed, a little sharply. "Don't overdo it," she said. "It's the old reverse-English technique, isn't it? Pretend you're not interested and they'll spill their guts. Particularly if you've gone to bed with them first."

I said, "Let's not make cracks about that. You can't help having the thought, but just keep it in your head, will you? I mean, you can talk things to death, you know."

Her eyes widened slightly. "I know," she murmured after a little pause. "I know. I'm sorry. You're really a pretty nice guy, aren't you?"

"Don't count on it."

"Hell," she said, "you've got to count on something. What kind of a life would it be if you didn't? There's a man here who worries me, Matt. He's working for Dad, and he scares me. He looks like. . . . well, he looks a little like you. I mean, he's about five inches shorter, and his hair is dark, and I'd never want to be alone in a room with him, but he's got the same—"

"The same what?"

She frowned. "I don't know. There's really no resemblance, now I think of it, but. . . . It's just a feeling, but somehow he reminds me of you. And Duke Logan. I bet he's got bullet-scars on him, somewhere. Watch out for him."

She reached out to touch my hand. "You see, I did stool-pigeon for you, just a little."

Chapter Ten

AFTER DINNER, we made the rounds of the gambling places. She was a roulette addict, which was nice for my simple mind. I never have understood the more complicated ways of losing money, like craps. As a matter of fact, I can't get much of a kick out of playing games where I know the odds are mathematically and inexorably against me—money games, that is. I played a few times, enough to make certain this wasn't the night I was meant to get rich; and then I just followed her around and watched her throw the stuff away.

What she did with her money didn't bother me, but she'd started drinking quite heavily, too, and you can never be sure, when they're young, just how much they know about their own capacities. I was tempted to warn her to slow down; but I had a hunch she was just waiting for me to make like a stern parent so she could inform me again that she was no teen-age kid, particularly not my teen-age kid, and that her alcoholic intake was none of my business. They're always so damn sensitive about their new-found adult independence, at that age. I kept my mouth shut and made each of my drinks last out two of hers, so that at least one of us would be able to find the way home when the time came. It was a long time in coming.

"Matt," she said abruptly, well on towards morning.

"Yes, kid?"

"Over by the pillar there. The man in the dark suit. I thought we might run across him, if we stuck it out long enough."

I didn't move at once. Then I picked up her white purse, took a cigarette from it, and a silver lighter with the initials M.F., for Moira Fredericks. I lighted a cigarette, took it from between my lips, and placed it between hers.

"Thanks, baby," she said. "Do you see him?"

I had him spotted, in the mirror inside the flap of the purse. "I see him," I said.

"That's the one."

She didn't have to tell me. I was looking at Martell. As usual, the picture and description I'd seen hadn't added up to anything much like the actual man. He had thick, black, glossy hair brushed straight back from his broad forehead, and a long mouth with thick, meaty, sexy lips— I remembered his weakness for women, that had cost him two official reprimands.

As Moira had said, he was wearing a dark suit, one of the few dark suits in the room. He had dark glasses on. It didn't make a damn bit of difference. He could have been wearing a mask and I would have known him. You learn to have a feeling for the people in your own line of business.

If you were working for a criminal organization, Mac had said, *you'd be called enforcers. . . . removers is a very good word.* Martell was playing both roles now, proving, I guess, that there isn't much difference in actual practice.

He was packing a shoulder gun, I noted, to go with his cover as Fredericks' bodyguard. Judging by his dossier, he'd be fast with it, as fast as you can be with a rig like that. Not that it mattered. We don't go in much for face-to-face showdowns. When the time came that he needed a gun on my account, he'd either have all the time in the world to get it out, or no time at all.

"A real attractive specimen," I said, closing the purse. It took a little effort to do that, and to leave my back to him. I found myself wishing I hadn't left the .38 back at the motel. There's only one answer to a good pistol-man, and that's another pistol. It's something they don't do so well across the water, where they tend to think of a handgun as just a portable rifle—sometimes they even equip them with folding stocks, for God's sake! They haven't got the fine old pistol traditions that we have. But

Martell had been playing gangster long enough to be thoroughly acclimatized, I was sure. "How long's he been working for your dad?" I asked.

"I don't know," she said. "Not very long, I think, but he was here when I got back from. . . . Don't pump me, Matt. I only pointed him out to you because. . . . well, because there's something about him that frightens hell out of me."

"I know," I said. "He reminds you of me. That would frighten hell out of anybody."

She looked up from the table and made a face at me. "Get me a drink, will you, baby?"

I hesitated. Her voice was steady enough, but she'd had a lot and her eyes showed it. Her hairdo, as always when it was subjected to stress, had come slightly unraveled—but only enough to look kind of cute and windblown, and in other respects she was still quite presentable. But I didn't know what another would do to her, and I didn't really want to find out. You never feel quite the same about someone you've had to mop up after.

Well, she wasn't my child, she wasn't my wife, and it was hard to say if I could even call her my girl. I went and got her the drink, noting that Martell had disappeared. I wondered if he'd recognized me. It seemed unlikely, unless he had special information. They wouldn't have much of a dossier on me yet. After all, I'd only been back in the organization a year. He'd been away from his master files a long time. He'd looked at me, to be sure, but, as Fenn, it would be part of his job to keep track of guys hanging around the boss's daughter. . . .

When I returned, Moira had left the wheel and was waiting by a potted palm nearby.

"Thanks," she said, and lifted the glass to her lips, and tasted the contents. Then she grinned at me over the rim, turned, and deliberately poured the liquor into the gravel at the base of the palm. "Okay, baby," she said. "That does it. You can stop worrying now."

"What have we been proving?" I asked.

"The books say it isn't hereditary," she answered, "but every now and then I kind of have to check up on the books—like after learning for sure my dear old daddy's a dope peddler."

"I never said—"

She paid me no attention. "Or am I insulting him by calling him that? I suppose his position is strictly administrative, and he never touches the nasty stuff with his own white manicured hands. That makes it much better, of course. That makes it just swell!" She swayed slightly, and steadied herself, and spoke in a totally different tone: "Jeeps, I'm starting to feel them, now I'm standing up. How do I look, ghastly?"

"No, but a comb wouldn't hurt."

She reached up. "The damn stuff's always falling down on me. I'll be right back. Stand by to carry out the body and revive it with black coffee." She took my hand and turned it so she could see my wristwatch. "My God, it's almost time for breakfast! Food? Ugh, what a horrible thought!"

We'd taken my truck, although it was less aristocratic than her open Mercedes, because Sheik would be more comfortable in it. The fact that I might not like a large hairy animal being comfortable among my bedding and camping gear obviously hadn't occurred to her. When she returned from making repairs—her hairdo neatly reconstructed for the second time that evening—we rode the elevator down, crossed the hotel parking lot in silence, and got into the pickup's cab.

"Where do you want this coffee?" I asked.

She hesitated. "Have you got some in that box of stuff in back? And a stove?"

"And water," I said, "but you're hardly dressed for a picnic."

She leaned against me sleepily. "You spend more time worrying about this damn dress!" she murmured, and grinned reminiscently. "Well, talking about it, anyway. Just turn right and keep going. I'll tell you when to turn again. . . ."

The transition from the gaudy night life of Reno to the dark, silent desert nearby, was almost shocking. Presently we were rolling across an arid landscape that might have been the surface of the moon or Mars, vaguely illuminated by the threat of dawn in the east. Following her instructions, I turned onto a dirt road leading back into the bleak, low hills. When there wasn't any sign of civilization around us, I stopped the truck, set the brake, and cut the lights and motor.

I wasn't really feeling very amorous, but common politeness seemed to indicate a kiss, at the very least, so I reached for her. She shook her head, holding me off.

"It's Fenn, isn't it?" she said.

I could barely see the white shape of her face, and her shadowy eyes watching me. "What's Fenn?" I asked.

"The man I pointed out to you. Jack Fenn. He's the one you're after, isn't he?"

I said, "Don't be too clever, Moira."

"You said you weren't really interested in Dad, and I believed you. So it had to be Fenn. So I showed him to you. You didn't give yourself away much, baby. Just a little." She licked her lips. "It was . . . kind of scary, watching you. Like a hawk or something. . . ." Then she was in my arms, holding me tightly, her face buried in my shoulder. Her voice was muffled. "Why couldn't we just be two ordinary people, with ordinary jobs and parents? Why does it have to be. . . . Why? That's a lousy, useless word, isn't it? You're really not after Dad, are you? But if he should get in the way . . ."

You had to hand it to the kid. She kept coming up with all the right answers. I'd met professionals who'd have taken a week to get the information she'd wormed out of me in one evening—and the funny thing was, the more she learned, the more sure I became that she was just exactly what she seemed. There was something naïve and direct about her prying that, more and more, led me to believe that my earlier suspicions had been unjustified.

She sat up beside me suddenly, looking through the windshield.

"What's the matter?"

"There's a jack," she said. "Look!"

She pointed, and I saw a long-legged jack rabbit take

off through the sparse brush. There was light around us now, although the sun was not yet in sight. Moira freed herself from my arm and reached for the door handle.

I said, "What—"

"I promised to show you something this morning, remember? Have you got a pair of binoculars in this caravan? Well, get them quick while I get the dog."

She was a screwy kid. I dug around behind the seat and got out the war-surplus 7x50's that I carry there—I picked up some fine, light, compact Leitz glasses overseas, but they're too nice to leave around like that; besides, they don't have the light-gathering power of the big old optical relic. When I came around the truck, she had Sheik out, at the cost of some paw-smudges on the front of her dress. While she brushed herself off, he was stretching lazily, looking completely ridiculous with his bony rump in the air and his long body flexed like Robin Hood's bow.

"Come on," she said. "Let's see if he'll pick it up."

We made a peculiar procession heading out across the desert, she in her high heels with the unlikely-looking dog on leash, and I following gingerly in my sporty loafers, carrying the binoculars, cased. I don't know if we found the same bunny or another—they're hares, actually —but suddenly there was a thumping sound and one took off ahead of us. Moira knelt down quickly and put her arm around the dog's neck as she snapped off the lead. She hugged him tightly and released him.

"Go get him, Sheik!" she breathed. "Go get him, big dog!"

The Afghan didn't pay much attention to this pep talk. He didn't seem much interested in the vanished jack rabbit, either. He just stood for a moment, kind of looking around vaguely and testing the breeze with his nose— why he'd bother with that, I don't know, since they're supposed to be sight-runners without much sense of smell. Maybe nobody'd told him.

Then he started forward deliberately with that gliding gait I'd seen once before. He didn't really seem to be gathering speed, any more than a train pulling out of the station so gradually, at first, that you don't realize it's moving. . . . By the time I realized Sheik actually had something in view and was going after it, he was lost to sight over the nearest ridge.

"This way!" Moira said. "Up on the knob here! We can see it all from there, I hope."

We labored upwards. The Nevada desert is a prickly place—maybe all of them are—and I kept getting small sharp spikes driven clear through the leather of my shoes. How she was doing in her thin pumps, I didn't even want to think about. We reached the top, panting, and looked around. There wasn't an animal visible that I could see.

"Let me have them," she said, taking the binoculars from me. "There he is!" she said presently, passing them back. "Look way out there. See, along that arroyo—"

The dog was out there, all right. I just hadn't looked far enough out. I found him with the naked eye, first. He didn't seem to be moving very fast, just kind of ambling along. Then I put the glasses on him, and drew my breath sharply. You hear loose talk about how beautiful deer are, running, but actually it's kind of a bunchy progress, if you know what I mean: great big muscles going off in great big explosions of power. This animal was running faster than any deer ever dreamed of, and he didn't seem to be expending any energy at all.

She spoke beside me. "He's not really traveling yet. They've been clocked at sixty. Wait till he cuts in the afterburners. . . . There! Now he's getting down to work. Watch!"

I'd almost forgotten she was there. I remembered my manners and started to pass her the binoculars.

She said, "No, you keep them. I've seen it. I'm going to sit down over there and get the prickles out of my feet. Tell me when he makes the kill."

I had the rabbit in sight now. The big jack was going flat out, running for his life, every muscle straining, and behind him came the lean gray dog, running silently, its long fur rippling with the wind of its own motion, its head well forward, its long hound ears streaming back. There was no strain here, no effort; there was just pale death flowing over the ground. . . . It was over in an instant, just a snap and a toss of the head. I started breathing again and turned away.

Moira looked up as I approached. "Did he get it?"

"Yes," I said. "He got it. My God!"

She smiled. "I told you I'd show you something." Her smile faded. "It's kind of horrible, actually, but it's what he was bred for, isn't it? Well, gazelles and things, but we're a little short of gazelles over here. It's what he was born for, if he was born for anything. You can't . . . you can't not let him do it, can you? I mean, it's the only thing he's really good at." She put her shoes back on and reached up to be helped to her feet. "Let's go back to the truck. He'll be out there a while, now. You can make the coffee while we wait."

She didn't want anything to eat. I hauled the mattress out of the truck bed for her to sit on comfortably while I worked with the Coleman stove on the tailgate. We had our coffee and watched the sun rise over the desert.

Moira said suddenly, "You're still in love with her, aren't you?" I looked at her quickly. She said, "Don't give me that stupid look, baby. You know what I'm talking about. I saw you out there at the ranch, the way you looked at her. That cold ice princess."

"She's not—" I checked myself.

"Not cold?" Moira laughed shortly. "Don't kid me, baby. I know these lovely, gracious ladies who hoard it like gold and restrict it like a private beach."

I wasn't going to discuss Beth's sexual attitudes with her. I said, "She's really a pretty fine person, Moira."

"Sure," Moira said. "The only trouble is, I loathe fine people."

"Particularly after they've kicked you out on your ear," I said maliciously.

She started to speak angrily; then she grinned. "Okay, maybe I am a little prejudiced." She sighed, leaning against me comfortably. "It's nice out here. I wish we didn't have to go back, ever. I wonder how many women have said that to how many men." After a while, she said, "You don't have to say you love me. I just want to know . . . you're going to be nice to me, aren't you? As nice as . . . as circumstances permit?"

It was something else I didn't particularly care to discuss. I said crudely, "You mean, right now?"

She glanced at me, startled. She even flushed a little. Then she laughed. "Well, it wasn't exactly what I had in mind, baby, but if you want . . ."

The dog stayed out just long enough, and then, while we were making ourselves more or less fit for civilization again, he came trotting in, grinning from ear to ear, and sat down to have the leash put on him. Moira got a wet rag and washed him off a bit—there was some gore that might have shocked her sensitive city neighbors— and we drove back to Reno.

I took her to the motel so she could pick up the Mercedes. I escorted her across the parking area, with the Afghan trotting alongside. That dog was hell on rabbits, but apparently he had no interest in humans. He didn't give the slightest warning. As a watchdog, he was a washout. I don't think he even knew they were around, until they jumped me from the bushes, and even then he seemed to figure it wasn't any of his damn business. Well, maybe he was right.

Chapter Eleven

WHEN THEY came at you like that, from behind, they never really expect you to be ready for them; and if you act fast and decisively, at precisely the right time, you can generally take care of one of them as you turn. The other—they practically always hunt in pairs, since nobody'd be fool enough to entrust just one with a responsible job—will generally run then, and you can let him go or pick him off as you choose.

I knew they were there, all right. I've been getting along on my own five senses, without any watchdogs to help me, for quite a while. The trouble was, they were so clumsy it was obviously the freshman team. Fenn apparently hadn't thought me worthy of his own attentions, if Fenn had sent them. Maybe he'd just reported to Fredericks that a certain long, lecherous drink of water was making eyes at his daughter, and Fredericks himself had called some unskilled labor off the street to do the job.

I took the chance that the awkward characters behind me hadn't been sent to do any shooting. They'd just been sent to issue an invitation, I hoped; and I might learn something by going along. I might also get hell kicked out of me—I wasn't forgetting what had happened to Paul—but on the whole I figured the biggest risk was that one of them might be sap-happy. You see so many TV shows these days in which people get beat over the head without deleterious results that the rising generation of punks tends to overestimate the durability of the human skull.

There was a very unpleasant moment while they closed in. I guess they thought they were moving with silent efficiency. I continued walking beside Moira. We paused by the car. She was saying something, I don't remember what. Maybe I didn't even hear it. My scalp had tightened up hard enough to pull my ears out of register, waiting for the blow to fall.

Then one of them had a gun jammed into my kidneys, and the other had danced around to threaten me with a long switch-blade knife. It was so childish I wanted to cry for them. Some day they'd do it to a man who didn't want to be taken, and they'd never be the same again.

"Don't move, Buster!" the knifeman said in a menacing voice. "Keep him covered, Tony!"

Tony kept me covered, while Switchblade folded his surgical implement, put it away, and searched me so efficiently that he didn't even spot the little Solingen knife in my pants pocket. Well, he was young. He'd learn, if he lived long enough, which didn't seem likely, or even desirable.

"Look out!" the man behind me warned him, and Switchblade turned just in time to catch a thrown white purse squarely across the face. He rubbed his nose and took a step forward angrily. The kid was ready for him, with her fists up, ready to take him on, and any three friends he might care to name. She'd apparently been something of a tomboy in her day. It must have been something to see. The one behind me said quickly, "Watch it, Ricky. If you lay a hand on her, The Man will have your hide!"

Moira said breathlessly, "Get him, Sheik! Get him, big boy! Get them both! Tear their lousy throats out!"

Switchblade Ricky took a quick step backwards, watching the dog. It opened its mouth lazily, showing the biggest, whitest teeth in the world; and the punk took another step back and reached into his pocket for the knife. The dog finished yawning and looked up at its mistress in a puzzled way: any fool could see there weren't any rabbits here.

Ricky laughed, but he'd been scared, he'd shown it, and he had to regain status. He stepped forward, bravely now, and kicked the dog hard. It cried out like a hurt child and slunk away to the end of the leash and cowered there with its long monkey tail between its legs, looking back over its shoulder with big, outraged, heartbroken eyes.

Moira gave a little cry, and knelt on the dusty pavement, and hugged the beast to her. "Oh, Sheik!" she moaned. "Oh, baby, I'm sorry, I shouldn't have . . . !" She looked up, kneeling there. "I'll kill you for that!" she breathed.

Tony, behind me, whose face I hadn't seen, said, "For Christ's sake, let's cut out the comedy. . . . Miss Fredericks, get in your car and go home." He cleared his throat and said a word that probably hadn't crossed his lips in years, if ever; they don't seem to teach it to modern youth much. "Please."

She glanced at me, standing there a helpless prisoner with the threatening gun in my back. "What are you going to do to him?"

Tony said, "It's got nothing to do with you, Miss. Big . . . I mean, Mr. Fredericks just said to bring him in. I'm just following orders, Miss."

"Well, we'll see about your lousy orders—"

I said, "It's all right, kid. Go on home."

She turned on me. "Don't you tell me what to do! What's the matter with you, letting these two lousy delinquents . . . ?" She stopped quickly, and looked at me sharply. She wasn't someone you had to draw blueprints for, labeled in red luminous ink. After a moment, she rose to her feet and said, "All right, but I'm coming along."

Switchblade Ricky said, "The hell you—"

"Save it," Tony said. "Miss Fredericks says she's coming, she's coming. How are you going to stop her, when she knows where we're going? Let The Man worry about it." He spoke to Moira. "Suit yourself, Miss Fredericks. But we can't give you a lift; it would be kind of crowded in one car with four of us and that big dog. . . . Come on, you!" he said, nudging me with his firearm.

We drove into town in a big Chrysler of some kind, with Ricky at the wheel and Tony in the back seat beside me, taking his duty as guard very seriously. I don't think I could have disarmed him more than half a dozen times during the trip. For a punk his age, with a prisoner of my age and experience, that was a pretty good performance. He was an underfed-looking specimen with too-long hair and too-loud clothes. The only thing you could say for him was that he was an improvement on Ricky, which wasn't really a high recommendation for anybody.

Moira's little Mercedes followed us closely all the way. Ricky stopped in a parking lot, and Moira pulled up alongside. Getting out, under Tony's gun, I discovered we were in the lot where I had parked the truck some hours earlier. Well, that figured, vaguely. Moira said good-bye to Sheik, and we all proceeded into the same hotel, although by a different door.

A private elevator bore us smoothly upwards, there was no telling how far. The door opened and let us out into an ordinary hotel corridor, like any other hotel corridor, except that there were a couple of men lounging on a leather sofa in a nearby alcove. One of them rose and came up.

"He's in the office, waiting," this man said. "What kept you?"

"We've been staked out at the motel, where her car was. They didn't get back until ten minutes ago," Tony said.

The man jerked his head towards Moira. "Who said anything about bringing her?"

"She did."

"Just a minute." The man went away and came back. He spoke to me. "This way. . . . You, too, Miss Fredericks." When the two youths who'd brought us started to follow, he gave them a look of surprise. "Who invited you? Stay here."

We walked down the corridor to an unmarked door. Our escort opened it and stepped back for Moira to enter. Then he shoved me in after her and closed the door behind us, remaining outside. There were two men awaiting us in the room. One I'd already seen elsewhere in this hotel. Martell was standing just to the left of the door.

One glance was enough to show that I'd made an error in judgment. He'd let Fredericks send a couple of juveniles to bring me in, all right, but it wasn't because he didn't know who I was or why I was there. His voice was very soft, reaching only to me and maybe the girl beside me. It was a smooth, cultured voice with a slight accent: not the voice of a gangster named Fenn.

"Greetings, Eric," he murmured. "Any friend of Paul's is welcome."

Well, anyway, I knew now why Paul had tried too hard to reach me before he died. He'd wanted to warn me that, under duress, he'd talked. He'd told all about me—and Martell was just the man to do something about the information, or get Fredericks to do it for him.

Chapter Twelve

MARTELL STEPPED BACK, to a point from which he could cover us safely, and it was time for me to forget him, for the moment, and turn my attention to the other man, sitting behind the desk.

He was a big man, a dark man, a man who'd have to shave twice a day and use plenty of talcum powder between times. He was an ugly man, with too-small features in a face that had spread out around them, particularly below the chin. He had a pug nose that I'd seen before, in a much refined and more attractive edition, but the mouth and eyes weren't familiar—she must have got those from her mother's side of the family, lucky girl.

"Hello, Dad," Moira said.

The funny thing was, my first feeling was a kind of embarrassment I hadn't felt in years, not since I was young enough to be taking girls to dances, after one of which we'd gotten bogged down on a dirt road where we'd had no business being—none that we cared to talk about, anyway—and it wasn't until close to four in the morning that I got my date home, muddy and disheveled, to find her parents awake and waiting.

This man was Big Sal Fredericks: he was a racketeer and worse, but he was also a father, and his daughter was standing beside me, after a night in my company, with her wonderful red-gold hair, as usual, tumbling down around her ears, with her expensive kid pumps ruined by rocks and thorns, with her smart piqué dress wrinkled and far from clean. Even her youthful resilience had its limits, and she'd passed them during the night. At least her costume had.

She looked very young like that, like a dressed-up baby at the end of a tough birthday party, and I was

76

ashamed of myself. I wouldn't have wanted another man to bring my daughter home like that—particularly not a man so much older than she was. There was a moment in which I really wanted to apologize, quite sincerely. But Sally Fredericks put me at ease at once.

He got up and looked at us. He walked around the desk and approached his daughter and looked her up and down. Then he struck her hard across the face with his open hand.

"You slut!" he said.

He turned to me. He used his fist on me. It was quite a punch, slow but with lots of power. I managed to roll with it or he might have broken my jaw. I went down. It seemed like a good idea to let him think he'd really hurt me, and as a matter of fact, he had. He still wasn't satisfied. He came over and kicked me hard in the side. Then he went back around the desk and sat down, rubbing his knuckles proudly.

After catching my breath, I looked at Martell, who jerked his head to let me know it was all right to get up. In a way, it was nice to be dealing with at least one professional. With amateurs, you've got to watch every minute that they don't do by mistake what they could never do on purpose. I know of at least one good operative, behaving himself perfectly, who was killed by a jittery farm boy with no more sense than to rest his finger on the trigger of a shotgun.

But with Martell around, you knew you'd never be killed accidentally—for what it was worth. I thought I could see a kind of malicious amusement in his eyes. He didn't mind a bit watching Fredericks work me over, knowing that, to stay in character, I had to take it meekly. . . . I got up and looked at the kid standing there with her hand to her cheek and hatred in her eyes, as she glared at her father, behind the desk.

"Who's this creep?" Fredericks demanded. "Another of those barflies you keep picking up? Haven't I told you—"

"You've told me," she said. She took her hand down, revealing a reddened area along the cheekbone that might go away, but might also color up into a real bruise. Her voice was level and cold and adult. "I'm supposed to stay home all day and watch TV."

"Nobody's talking about what you do in the day!"

"All night, then," she said.

"I warned you what I'd do to any jerk who——" He drew a long breath, and said, "I've tried to do what I should. I've tried to be both parents to you since your mother——"

"Let's not bring Mother into this!"

He said, "I've sent you to the best schools, given you money and clothes and cars, and what do you do? First you get yourself mixed up with a married fellow and then you come back here and shame me by trying to act like the town tramp—my daughter! Why didn't you stay back east like I told you and find yourself some nice socialite fellow your own age——"

"I did," she said, "but you know, it's funny how they always seemed to lose interest when they learned my dad was Sal Fredericks, the big hotel man. I guess there's kind of a prejudice against the hotel business these days."

He flushed, and controlled himself. "Why do you do it, baby?" he asked, and for a moment he was human and I could feel a little sorry for him. "Why do you do it? Look at you, my daughter that I've tried to bring up nice, like a lady, standing there looking like you'd been sleeping in your clothes——"

"I have," she said bluntly. "With him. Twice."

We weren't there any longer, Martell and I. They were alone in the room, the two of them, swinging at each other with spiked clubs, drawing real blood. She didn't look at me as she said it, and he didn't look at me as he heard it; he'd get to me later.

"Why, baby?" he asked again.

"Because he was the only man I could find who had the guts! Who wasn't scared of you!"

"We'll see about his guts," Fredericks said. "Now you go home and clean yourself up——"

She said, "You're not going to touch him! You're not going to lay a finger on him!"

He said, "Fenn, take her home!"

There was a slight hesitation. I didn't look in Martell's direction.

He said, "Mr. Fredericks, I don't think I ought to leave right now."

"What the hell do you. . . . Oh, this one? Hell, I can handle this beanpole Casanova. You saw—"

"Yeah, I saw," Martell said, and I knew he was squirming inside like a hooked angleworm. He didn't want to leave. He wanted to stay and supervise my fate. But it was his turn to remain in character. He tried once more, however. "My advice—"

Fredericks flushed. "Who the hell's asking your advice, punk? Take her home. And, Fenn. . . ."

Martell's voice was very soft. "Yes, Mr. Fredericks?"

"Don't go inside the door. I heard all about you long before you got here."

"Yes, Mr. Fredericks."

He came across the room stiffly. Moira seemed to come out on her hate dream with a start. The mark of her father's hand was still red on her cheek, but her eyes were suddenly dark and remorseful as she glanced in my direction.

She'd used me to hurt the man behind the desk, without thinking of me. Now she was realizing what she'd done to me—or thought she'd done: the outcome hadn't really been changed much by her angry words. Fredericks hadn't brought me here to welcome me into the family.

I said, "Run along, kid."

"I won't leave—"

"Go on," I said, wishing she'd hurry up and get Martell out of there. As long as he was around, I was in serious trouble.

"I'm sorry," she breathed. "I didn't mean. . . . I just kind of flipped, I guess."

"Sure. Now go."

She started to speak again, and checked herself. Martell was waiting. She went up to him, and they left the room together. Before the door closed, I saw a man standing guard outside, the man who'd brought us down the hall.

It still wasn't good, but with Martell gone it didn't worry me too much. I'd met Fredericks; I knew where I stood with Martell; I'd learned all I could expect to learn here. It was time to stage a disengagement, as we used to say in the Army.

Fredericks was staring at me hard over the desk. He said, "So you've got guts, have you? We'll see about your guts!"

I watched him get up and walk around the table and come to me, and I couldn't help being aware of my aching ribs and throbbing jaw. These hoodlums walk so big and talk so loud.

He said, "That isn't the only thing we'll see about. We'll fix you so you'll be no more trouble to young girls."

It wasn't unexpected, it was the way his mind would work, but it didn't help establish him in my mind as a citizen to be protected and preserved. He came to me and slapped me across the face—slapped me, for God's sake! It was pitiful. It was irritating. You get tired of being the cold, impersonal, machine-like hunter of men sometimes; you think of the fun it would be to do one strictly for kicks. . . .

My hand was in my pocket, and the little knife was in my hand. He slapped me again, and I'd had enough of Salvatore Frederici, and I grinned at him pleasantly, the little man who was dead and didn't know it. All I had to do was bring it out, flick it open, and insert it in the right place. By any standards of judgment, he'd lived quite long enough. My mind gave the signal. My hand didn't move. I couldn't do it.

I couldn't do it. I heard Mac's voice: *It's a war of sorts and you can consider yourselves soldiers of sort. . . .* I couldn't do it just because I was fed up with the guy. I couldn't do it because he'd slapped Moira. I couldn't even do it because, in some way that I didn't know about yet, he was undoubtedly the man responsible for turning the ranch where my children lived into an armed camp with an atmosphere of terror.

Don't misunderstand me. He was on the list, and if I ever got a chance at him in the line of duty, I wouldn't hesitate. In fact, from now on I'd be looking for the chance. But I didn't need to kill him to get away—at least I didn't think so—and I couldn't kill him just because he'd made me lose my temper. It wasn't a sufficient reason. It wasn't what I'd been trained for. It wasn't what I was here for, to avenge injuries to my tender pride. . . .

Chapter Thirteen

SOMETHING moved in his eyes, a kind of sudden, vague uneasiness, and he stepped quickly to the desk and hit a buzzer. An instant later the man in the hall was standing behind me. There was a little more after that, of course. Big Sal had been afraid for a moment there; and like his boy Ricky he had to regain status by kicking the dog. I had a tender abdomen and a bloody nose to add to my souvenirs when they marched me out and turned me over to the two punks, with instructions. Ricky thought those instructions were real great.

"Keep him covered," he said to Tony. "Keep the bastard covered till we get him out of town where I can work on him right."

Tony said, "Do you just give orders around here, or can you push elevator buttons, too?"

They took me downstairs again, and out across the parking lot to the car. It was broad daylight now, and had been for several hours, and I had that feeling of having lost track of the days that comes when you've gone without sleep for a while. It was hot, with the dry Nevada heat bouncing off the asphalt pavement. There were some people on the street but none in the parking area. The people who made this a busy place at night were sleeping late this morning. I didn't want any interference, so I waited until Tony had escorted me around the car before I took him.

I'd been a good boy long enough. He was nice and relaxed now, in exactly the right position. I got him by the arm and made the throw in fine style, bringing his arm down sharply across my knee at the finish. He screamed once as various anatomical items tore and snapped; then he hit the pavement with his head and was quiet. It was a little drastic and I felt a little sorry. Unlike some of them, Tony hadn't seemed to be working full time on being as big a louse as possible.

The gun had hit the pavement without going off, which was a relief. It had bounced under the car, which was all right. I didn't want it, anyway. I had other, less noisy, plans for Switchblade Ricky.

He'd been about to open the car door for us. He turned at the single, cut-off scream, and there was a comical, shocked look on his face as he realized that his partner was out of action and he was on his own. The knife came out fast, I'll hand him that. He pushed the button, and the long, thin blade clicked into place.

"All right for you, Buster," he said in his best, menacing tone. "You want it here, you can have it here, the full treatment!" He started forward.

I took my hand out of my pocket and gave the little snap of the wrist that flicks that kind of knife open if you keep it properly cleaned and oiled and know the technique. Opening it two-handed is safer and more reliable, but it doesn't impress people nearly so much. Tony's eyes widened slightly, and he stopped coming. This wasn't supposed to happen. When you pulled knives on suckers and squares, they turned pale green and backed off fearfully; they didn't come up with blades of their own.

He hesitated, saw that my cutting implement was only about half the length of his, regained confidence, and came in fast. I was tempted to play with him a bit, but it was hot, I was tired and sleepy, and when you start playing cat-and-mouse with human beings you deserve trouble and sometimes get it. I sidestepped his clumsy thrust, moved inside the knife, clamped a good hold on his arm, and made one neat surgical cut. The knife dropped from his fingers. That made two of them who'd be operating left-handed for a while, if not forever.

He backed off, holding his wrist, staring at the blood pumping from between his fingers.

I said, "You'd better get a tourniquet on that before you bleed to death."

I stepped over and put my foot on the blade of his

knife and pulled up on the handle until the steel snapped.
It didn't seem to be very good steel. I kicked the pieces
towards him.

"The cheaper the punk," I said, "the longer the
blade."

I backed away until I was fairly sure he couldn't hit
me left-handed even if he had a gun and came out of his
trance long enough to use it. I turned and walked away
across the parking lot, taking out my handkerchief to
wipe my little knife clean before putting it away. Then
I looked up, as a small open car that I recognized came
off the street in a hard flat turn that would have had an
ordinary sedan wallowing and screeching. I stopped
where I was and waited for her to reach me. She flung the
right-hand door open.

"Get in! Quick!"

"What's the rush?" I asked in a puzzled voice. I mean,
she was a pretty girl I'd spent the night with, and I'm
not superhuman.

She stared at me for a moment, and looked at the
knife and at the stains on the cloth with which I was
wiping it in a leisurely manner. Then she looked across
the area to where one man lay unconscious on the
ground and another stood leaning against a car, clutching
his wrist and watching the blood run out.

She said, "Damn you, stop grandstanding and get in
before somebody else comes out here!" I got in. She
swung the little Mercedes around sharply, and sent it
away. "Are you . . . all right?" she asked, looking straight
ahead.

"Yes."

"What were they going to do to you?"

"An operation was mentioned, I believe, among other
things."

She swallowed hard. "How lousy can you get?" Then
she said harshly, "Well, if there's a way of getting lousier,
he'll find it!"

Then she gave me a sudden, startled, questioning look,
and I realized what she was thinking: she'd left me alone

with her father—a prisoner—and she'd found me down here, walking free.

I said, "It's all right, Moira. Your dad's all right."

"Did I ask? Do I give a damn?"

I said, "Lousy as he is, he's still your louse, you said once."

She started to speak angrily; then she sighed. "Sure. Blood is thicker than water and all that crap. The hell of it is, it's true. I could never feel the same. . . ." She glanced at me, flushed, and stopped. After a moment, she said, changing the subject completely: "You haven't asked me about my trip."

"Tell me about your trip."

"That's a real creep, from Creepville."

"I know," I said. "He reminds you of me."

She made a face at me. "Fenn," she said, tasting the word. It didn't taste good. "He didn't say a word out of line. He didn't touch me. But *think?* My God, he had me raped once a block and twice at each traffic light. He's got it on his mind so bad he aches all over. I'd hate to be working in the house that gets his business."

It was a matter of record, of course, but I was glad to have it confirmed from the feminine viewpoint.

"I was damn glad when the car that had been tailing us pulled up to pick him up," she said. "I was afraid he'd come into the house with me in spite of Dad's orders. I waited until they were out of sight, and jumped back in the Merc and drove like hell. . . . I hope Sheik's all right, alone there. Baby, do you think it's safe to go home?"

I considered the question briefly. Martell might want to come right after me again, but I doubted that Fredericks would let him. "I'd say so. I gave myself away pretty badly when I took those punks. Your dad will spot it as professional work."

She glanced at me. "Professional. I don't suppose I'd better ask what profession."

"You'd better not," I said. "I might tell you."

"I still think you're a government man. Even if—"

"Even if what?"

She shook her head. "I don't know. I guess I don't want to know. How does your giving yourself away make it safe for us to go home?"

"Your dad acted hastily and lost a couple of his boys, at least temporarily. He won't want to make the same mistake again. He'll guess I'm not just an amorous tourist, and he'll want to do some serious investigating before he takes further action."

"You hope," she said, "because here we are."

We pulled into the driveway by the little blue house and went inside, picking up the newspaper that lay on the front step. I had again that funny feeling of guilt. I was bringing my girl home in broad daylight after a long and dissipated night.

The dog had a nice padded wicker bed by the little fireplace at the end of the living room. He acknowledged our presence, after the door had closed behind us, by opening one eye to look at us warily and closing it again with relief: we weren't the kicking variety of humans.

"Some watchdog," I said. "I read somewhere that they were even used to hunt leopards back where they came from, but I guess the modern breed is pretty much for show and rabbits. It's funny how they can breed the guts out of just about any animal, if they keep at it long enough."

I was teasing her, and she reacted right away: "You're not being fair! Just because he wouldn't. . . . I asked too much of him. He just didn't understand!"

"Maybe not," I said, "but I'd sure hate to stack him up against a real tough bobcat, and they only weigh about thirty pounds. . . . All right, all right," I said, grinning, as she threatened to become violent. "He's a big brave dog and he just didn't want to hurt those poor little fellows. . . . Ouch!"

She'd kicked me. I grabbed her, and we wrestled a bit, not altogether playfully. She was really mad. Then, her temper vanished in an instant, and she was laughing, and then she gasped, and I looked where she was looking at our images in the big mirror by the door: two beat-up characters too long without sleep, too long in their clothes. She freed herself and faced the mirror squarely.

"Oh, my God!" he said. "No wonder Dad said . . ."

She checked herself, grimaced, reached down for the belt and back for the zipper, and let the dress fall about her feet. She stepped out of it and kicked it through the open bedroom door and one shoe with it. She kicked the second shoe after the first, and reached up to extract the few remaining pins from her hair, shaking it loose. It was longer than I'd thought, soft and bright to her bare shoulders.

"Look," she said, still prospecting for pins, "why don't you start some eggs and coffee while I take a shower; then I'll get breakfast on the table while you're cleaning up. . . . What's the matter?" She glanced down at herself, barefoot, in brassiere and panties, and said impatiently, "Oh, for God's sake, you've made love to me twice! So I've got a body. Big deal!"

I said, grinning, "Who's impressed? Go take your damn shower."

She said, "Baby—" The doorbell rang. She said, with another glance at her brief costume, if you could call it that, "Oh, damn. Get that, will you, baby?"

I gave her time to withdraw into the bedroom and close the door. Then I opened the front door. The man outside was wearing clean coveralls and a cap with some kind of public utilities insignia. He was carrying one of those aluminum-covered notebooks or clipboards they use. He said something I didn't catch, and opened the cover of the thing to show me something. When I stepped forward, his partner, whom I hadn't seen, came up from my left and hit me over the head with a sap.

Chapter Fourteen

ALL RIGHT, so it was a stupid damn business, and if I'd seen it on TV I'd have groaned and turned off the set with, perhaps, some comments on the silly behavior of the supposedly tough and competent private eye on the screen, walking right into it like that. All I can say is that I'd had two nights without sleep, the last one a real dilly; I wasn't at my best. Of course, we hardly ever are, in times of crisis. Unlike Olympic athletes, lucky fellows, we don't get to go into training for our major efforts, with plenty of good wholesome food and lots of sleep. We're supposed to do it on benzedrine and hard liquor if necessary, which it usually is.

Anyway, they caught me completely off guard, the way a man like me isn't ever supposed to be. I thought I had the opposition all figured out; and the time you start thinking that is the time you usually find out you're wrong. I won't say that the fact that I went to the door with my mind less on who might be out there than on my bright mental image of the kid without too many clothes on didn't have something to do with my negligence.

The sap-man was an expert. His blow was no harder than necessary, and no softer, either. I went down. The one in the coveralls kept me from hitting my face on the brick steps. I wasn't out, not completely; I was aware of the other man putting his instrument away—a cosh, it might have been called by Duke Logan, and why he came into my mind at that moment I didn't know. The two men between them dragged me into the house. They dumped me on the nearby sofa. I could see it all quite clearly although my eyes were closed. It was as if I was way out and above it somewhere, looking into the tiny toy house with its tiny toy living room and the tiny toy figures going through their minuscule motions.

"Did you have to hit him so hard?" a voice asked. "If you've killed him—"

"I don't kill them unless I'm paid to kill them," another voice said. "What did you want me to do, read his damn gas meter? What the hell's a *man* doing here, anyway?" It wasn't the voice of anybody I'd ever met. It went on irritably: "There was only supposed to be the girl and the dog. Keep an eye on the mutt while I look around; and on this character, too, in case he starts to—"

A third voice called, "Matt, who was it, baby?"

I was supposed to do something, and for the second time that day I couldn't do it. I didn't even know what it was, this time. I only knew that it was terribly important, that terrible things would happen if I didn't do it, but I couldn't move. I heard a door open somewhere.

"Matt, I—" Her voice changed. "Who the hell are you? What are you doing here?"

Then the door slammed shut again. Footsteps crossed the room towards it, fast, and a shoulder burst it open before she could get it locked. There was a scuffle in the other room and a man's voice called:

"Lou, for Christ's sake, come here and get the gun from the damn little wildcat before she. . . . Ouch! You bitch!"

There was the sound of a blow and a gasp of pain. The other man had gone in to help and I was alone, but not quite alone. Something new had come into the room. It was like one of those nightmares you have as a kid, when there's something big and black in the corner, growing, spreading, and if it ever touches you, you're gone. It was there, quite still at first and then moving, and I wanted to cry out, to warn them. After all, for all their faults, they were human beings like me. But I couldn't speak.

It flowed soundlessly towards the bedroom door, and after that the real nightmare began, with sound effects straight from hell, and the kid was in there, and I had to get to her, and I fell off the sofa trying, and passed out.

"Matt! Matt, please wake up!"

I came back from far away and opened my eyes. She came into focus in two places. The two images fused, and you've never seen anything like it. I mean, she looked like she'd been painting the house, only it wasn't paint. It brought me up sitting, even though I thought my head would kill me.

"Moira!" I gasped. *"Kid—"*

She said, "Oh, for God's sake don't make a federal case of it! It's just a little blood. It . . . it isn't mine. I'm all right."

I looked at her, and saw that she really was all right even if she looked ready to go on the warpath. The room started to revolve around me. She grabbed me as I swayed, sitting there.

"Please, baby!" she said. *"Please* try!"

"Try what?"

"You've got to come! He's in there. He's—" Her voice broke. "He's hurt. He's so terribly hurt! You've got to come and see if there's anything . . . anything you can do. Please, baby, *please* try to stand up!"

I tried to stand up. I made it. She helped me across the room to the bedroom door. After that, my head cleared very suddenly. I didn't even have a headache any more, or if I had, I couldn't be bothered with it.

The one nearest the door had tried to ward it off with his arm. It had sheared off the arm just below the elbow—well, that was the general impression I got, anyway—and had gone on for the throat. It had done a very thorough job there. The other one had apparently been trying to do some shooting. It hadn't bothered with the hand or the gun. It had just taken him by the neck, like the rabbit. The angle of the head indicated that a couple of vertebrae might actually be crushed or broken. There didn't seem to be any point in investigating more closely, however, since there wasn't much left between head and shoulders, anyway.

I must confess that I'm not an expert on really mangled bodies. We fought a secret war, one that didn't often confront us with the more gruesome effects of bombs and high-explosive shells. This was just about as messy a situation as I'd ever witnessed, and I had to gulp a couple of times to get my digestive tract operating in the right direction again. The kid paid no attention to the horrors on the floor.

"Over here," she said. "Quick!"

I went around the bed. The big dog was lying there, stretched out on his side. He was fairly gruesome, too; you can't go messing with carotids and jugulars without getting a little gory. She'd cleaned off his head, however. Apparently that was how she'd got it all over her, handling him. He tried to raise his head as we came up. The tip of his long tail moved. I'd seen him do lots of things with that silly monkey tail, but this was the first time I'd seen him wag it like a real dog. You could see that he was kind of proud of himself. He thought he'd done pretty well. He kept an eye on us, though; you could never be sure, if you were a dog, what these odd humans were going to approve of.

Moira went to her knees and took the lean gray head in her lap. The mouth opened, and I could see—and for the first time really appreciate—the long, cruel fighting jaw and the big, white, leopard-killing teeth. The dog started licking Moira's hand. I just stood there. I mean, how do you apologize to a dog?

"Easy, Sheik, easy," Moira said. She looked up at me pleadingly. "What do you think?"

I bent down and looked him over. He'd taken at least three bullets, one far back that had gone clear through from side to side, presumably while he was disposing of the first man, one diagonally into the chest as he turned, and one squarely into the chest, with powder burns, as he made his final charge right into the muzzle of the gun.

"What do you think?" Moira whispered. "Is there . . . anything we can do for him?"

There wasn't any sense in trying to fool her. "Just one thing," I said. "You'd better go into the other room."

Her eyes widened indignantly. "Go into. . . . you mean, *leave* him? What do you think I am?" She looked down, and scratched the dog gently between the long hound ears. It never took its eyes from her face. She spoke again without looking up. "Go on, damn you! What are you waiting for? Quick, before he moves and hurts himself some more!"

I did it, never mind how. She made it a little awkward, sitting there holding him, but it's something I'm good at, and I did a clean and satisfactory job. She sat there for a while longer with the head in her lap. She was crying helplessly, the tears streaming down her cheeks unheeded. Presently I went into the bathroom and started the shower running. Then I went back and picked her up and walked her in there and shoved her under the water, underwear and all. Sentiment is all very well, but she could grieve just as hard without looking like a major war casualty.

I got aspirin from the medicine cabinet, swallowed three tablets with water, and waited to make sure she'd be all right in there. After a little, some wet lingerie came flying over the frosted glass shower door, barely missing me. If she had that much strength, she'd live, and I found a sponge and mopped up what she'd tracked across the living-room rug. There wasn't anything to be done to the charnel house that had been a bedroom, short of a complete redecoration; I just closed the door on that.

When I returned to the bathroom, she was still in the shower. At the lavatory, I took care of the deficiencies in my own appearance as well as soap and water could. A razor would have been nice, and she had one, but I could find no spare blades, and I'd been married too long, once, to entrust my face to an edge that a woman had used on her legs and armpits. I went into the kitchen to start breakfast, which may seem callous, but the situation required some heavy thinking, and I don't think well on an empty stomach. I didn't figure the kid's digestion was the kind to be permanently inhibited by grief and horror, either.

Waiting for the stuff to cook, I glanced at the front page of the newspaper we'd brought inside. One column

was headed *Radioactivity Claims Two at Los Alamos.*
The paper reminded its readers that a technician had
just died locally, and said investigations were being made
to determine if certain installations weren't being just a
bit careless with the hot stuff. I read the piece to the
end and decided it wasn't a nice way to die, but then,
what is? I heard Moira's voice call to me.

"Matt, where are you?"

I laid the paper aside, and went into the living room.
She was standing at the door of the second bedroom—
the bathroom was between the two—drying her hair. I
went up to her. She was quite an intriguing sight, clean
and shining. She looked at me, and down at herself, and
grinned. It was a little weak, but it was a real grin.

"Well, I can't help it!" she said defensively. "All my
clothes are in . . . in there, and I just couldn't bring myself . . ." Her grin faded, and her eyes were suddenly
wet. "Poor Sheik. He was . . . so lovely, and so shy,
and such a clown. And so brave, when he really understood that somebody was hurting me."

If she could talk about it, it was going to be all right.
I said, "If you'll tell me what you need and where it
is, I'll go in and get—"

I stopped. She wasn't listening to me. She was looking
towards the front door. I turned. We hadn't heard a
sound. They must have left it slightly ajar when they
hauled me inside. Now it was open, and Beth was there.

Chapter Fifteen

YOU HAD TO hand it to the kid. She didn't do any silly, self-conscious, September-Morn stunts with the towel. She just kept right on drying her hair. After all, it was her house, and if she wanted to entertain gentlemen in her living room without any clothes on, it was her business.

"I'd appreciate it," she said, "if you'd close the door, Mrs. Logan. From either side."

Beth said dryly, "Yes, I can see how you might feel a slight draft, Moira."

She stepped inside and pushed the door closed behind her. She looked slim and kind of elegant, although she wasn't really dressed up. She was wearing a white silk shirt or blouse—I never have learned how they make the distinction—with her monogram on the pocket: E for Elizabeth. She'd been Beth to me but I remembered that she was Elizabeth to Logan. Her skirt was nicely tailored of some fine khaki material, or maybe the stuff is called chino when it joins the aristocracy. Her legs were bare, which always seems a pity to me; but the stocking business is dormant throughout that country all summer. She had enough of a tan to get by with it; and her neat, polished, saddle-leather pumps did nice things for her ankles.

She had her white Stetson on. Combined with the practical material of her skirt, it gave her an outdoorsy, western look. Apparently she was taking herself quite seriously, these days, as the lady of the ranch. I couldn't help thinking it was too bad he couldn't take her back to the family estate, if any, in old England; she'd have had lots of fun dressing up in tweeds, and she'd have looked swell in them, too.

"Did you want to see me about something, Mrs. Logan?" Moira asked.

Beth said, "If I did, I picked the right time, didn't I, dear? For seeing you, I mean. . . . Actually, I was looking for Mr. Helm. I started to knock and the door swung—"

"There's a bell, honey," Moira said. "You know, an electrical device operated by a small white button. What made you think you'd find Mr. Helm here?"

It was a good question. Beth didn't answer. I was shocked to see her standing there, obviously caught, like a schoolgirl, in a barefaced lie. It takes practice to become a good liar and she'd never given the subject much attention. She'd had an awkward question thrown at her, and she'd tossed out a phony answer without thinking, and now she was stuck with it. She obviously didn't know how she'd known she'd find me here. In fact, she hadn't known she'd find me here at all.

Moira didn't smile or show any visible signs of triumph. "Well, I'll leave you to discuss your business with Mr. Helm," she murmured.

Now, at last, she wrapped the big towel casually about her, before turning away. It was impeccable strategy. A woman's rear leaving the room naked never looks very dignified. I followed her into the bedroom. She turned on me fast.

"God damn it, get her out of here before I scratch her lousy eyes out!"

"Relax, kid," I said. I looked around. "What about the neighbors?"

"What do you mean?"

"Guns have been fired. Men have been torn to bloody shreds by wild beasts—"

"Ah, think nothing of it. We're all air-conditioned, hadn't you noticed? Anyway, if St. Peter were to blow his trumpet, those biddies would just gripe about that inconsiderate little trollop in the blue house turning her TV up too high. . . ." Moira drew a long breath. "What the hell does she want here, anyway?"

"I don't know," I said. "But I think it would be a good idea to find out, don't you?"

She glanced at me, hesitated, and said, "That depends, baby."

"On what?"

"On whose side you're on."

I looked down at her for a moment, and she looked right back with those sea-green, grown-up eyes. I took her face in my hands and kissed her on the forehead.

She let her breath go out softly. "Well, all right!"

I asked, "Do you want me to get you some things from the other room?"

"Skip it. She's got me so mad I could wade through dead bodies knee deep. You'd better get out there and entertain her. . . . Matt."

"Yes?"

"Don't make a habit of it, baby. What the hell good is a kiss on the *forehead,* for God's sake!"

I grinned and went out of the room. Beth had laid her western hat aside. Without it she wasn't Elizabeth of the Double-L Ranch any more; she was just a slender attractive woman to whom I'd once been married. Her light-brown hair looked smooth and soft. She was looking at a bookshelf, obviously cataloguing the kid's literary tastes for future reference. She turned as I came up.

"Matt," she said gently, "I'm surprised at you. That child!"

I said, "All available evidence proves she isn't, including, I believe, her birth certificate. Anyway, it's really none of your business now, is it, Beth? As I recall, you said it was a mistake and we shouldn't repeat it."

"No," she said. "I was just a little surprised, that's all, seeing you here."

"That's not the way you said it the first time. You said you'd come here to find me, remember?"

She smiled ruefully. "I know. It was silly of me, wasn't it."

"Have you thought of a better story?"

She said, "Well, no, I—"

"Of course, as a last resort, there's always the truth. What the hell *are* you doing here, Beth?"

She said, "Why, I—" Then she laughed. "You know, it's funny to be called that again. He calls me Elizabeth, you know."

"I know," I said. "Talking of surprises, think of the one I got, discovering you married to the former bodyguard of Sally Fredericks, a very competent gent packing an automatic pistol in a well-fitting shoulder holster. Considering the reasons you left me—"

She winced. "I know it must seem strange. I—"

She stopped. The kid was coming towards us from the open bedroom door. She'd put on sandals, a pair of plaid shorts—quite snug and predominantly blue—and a crisp white short-sleeved shirt, worn outside the shorts. Under other circumstances, I might have said it looked like a boy's shirt. With her inside it, the resemblance wasn't noticeable. Her hair was still damp about her head, and she'd got a dry towel with which to work on it some more.

She said, "Did I hear my dad's name being taken in vain?"

I had to think back to recall that Sally Fredericks had been mentioned. I said, "We were actually speaking of his one-time best boy, the Duke of Nevada."

"Ah, the Duke," Moira said, rubbing her head energetically. She turned to Beth. "I think we should have him in here, don't you, Mrs. Logan? He must be getting lonesome, waiting out in the car, or wherever he is, waiting for you to make your report."

Beth frowned. "I don't know what you mean. Larry isn't—"

The kid lowered the towel. Her bright hair was a wild, tumbled mess about her head, but suddenly she didn't look very cute or particularly funny; even if she had, the expression in her eyes would have kept anyone from laughing.

"I'm surprised at the Duke," she said softly. "Sending his wife. . . . He must be getting old. I guess he just can't take it any more." She was watching Beth with dangerous intentness. "Can *you* take it, Mrs. Logan?"

I asked, "Kid, what are you driving at?"

She wheeled on me. "Where are your brains, baby? Okay, you were married to her once, does that mean you have to stop thinking when she walks in the room? What's she doing here? Haven't you figured it out yet? They didn't want you, did they? I heard them talking; they were surprised to find you here—just as she was! That means they didn't come from Dad. He wouldn't send anybody after *me*. If he wants me, all he has to do is pick up the phone. I'm not scared of him; I'll come. He certainly wouldn't send a couple of goons to rough me up; he reserves that privilege for himself! Well, who else could have sent them but Duke Logan, hitting back at Dad for something? He's still got friends who'd do it for the Duke. But they didn't come back, and he's getting old and cautious I guess, and he's pretty well known around town, so after waiting awhile he sent his wife in here to scout around cautiously and find out what went wrong. . . . Isn't that right, Mrs. Logan?"

She'd swung back to face Beth, who licked her lips. "I don't know what you—"

Moira had her by the arm. Before I understood what she was about, the two of them were at the bedroom door—the closed one. Moira turned the knob with her free hand, kicked the door open, and gave Beth a hard push.

"Can you take it, Mrs. Logan? Take a good look and go make your damn report!"

Chapter Sixteen

WHEN BETH came back from the bathroom, the kid had arranged a little tableau for her. I was sitting on the living-room sofa, and she was sitting crosslegged on the floor between my feet, and I was working on her hair with the towel. We must have looked quite cozy and domestic.

Beth came in looking pretty good, considering. She'd pulled herself together nicely; she just had the pale, shaken, slightly disheveled look of anyone who's just lost a meal down the drain. She stopped in the doorway to look at us, and I thought she winced slightly—I guess it's always hard to face the fact that anyone you've lived with for years can be happy with somebody else, doing all the things you used to do together, and maybe a few more besides.

Moira said, "I poured some coffee for you, Mrs. Logan. I think it's still hot. . . . Ouch, take it easy, baby!"

Beth stood there looking at us for a moment longer. Something else was on her mind now; she looked kind of lost and bewildered.

"Coffee?" she said. "How can you. . . ?" She glanced towards the closed door, and away. "Shouldn't we . . . *do* something?"

"What?" I asked. "Only God can do what they really need done."

"But—"

I said, "They'll keep. For a while at least." She winced again at my crudity, as she was supposed to do. It was time she woke up to the fact that she was in the big league now. She'd been in it before, of course, but she hadn't known about it until the very last. This time she'd married into it from choice, unless the Duke had deceived her about his background, and he looked like

99

the kind who'd be honorable as hell about things like that. I said, "Something has to be done, sure, but when I do it, I want to know it's right. Sit down and drink your coffee, Beth."

I indicated a chair. She hesitated, and went quickly over and sat down. After a moment, she picked up the cup and saucer from the small table nearby and began to sip the coffee gingerly.

I said, "They *were* friends of the Duke's, weren't they?"

She didn't look up. "Please call him Larry," she said. "He's . . . trying to live down that other name and everything that went with it. Yes, they were his friends, or at least men he'd known when . . ." She stopped.

"When he was in the rackets," I said.

"Yes." Nobody said anything for a while. Beth lifted her head abruptly. "You have to understand. It was the children. He threatened to—"

"Who threatened?"

"Her father. Fredericks."

"Threatened to what?"

She looked at her coffee cup. "Terrible things. He was using the children—my children—as a club against Larry, to make him—"

"To make him what?" I asked when she stalled again. She shook her head quickly. "I can't tell you that."

I passed it up, and said, "Logan's had a boy of his own for years. He's been vulnerable to that kind of threat for years. And if he's anything like the man I think he is, he'd know the way to deal with it."

She shook her head quickly. "He hasn't had *me* for years. Fredericks thought I . . . I'd weaken and put pressure on . . ." She was silent for a little while. Then she said breathlessly, "He was right! Oh, he was absolutely right! I couldn't stand it. Not knowing what might be happening when they were out of my sight for even a moment. . . . You saw the way it was out there. I was going crazy!"

"So the Duke decided to relieve the pressure?"

Beth hesitated, and glanced at Moira, and burst out,

"Why should *she* be immune? If he can threaten *my* children—"

I said, "Well, it didn't work. It's kind of too bad. I don't figure the two goons were any great loss, but that was a damn nice dog."

Beth's head came up sharply. She looked at me, a glance of sheer horror. I wasn't showing the proper respect for human life. Well, it was time she got used to that.

I said, "There's just one thing everybody seems to have overlooked." Neither of them was obliging enough to feed me the proper question. Suddenly I felt old and sad and tired. I said, "Those are my children, too. If Duke Logan can't protect them properly, I guess I'll have to." Nobody said anything to that, either. I gave the kid's head a last vigorous rub, and dropped the towel over her face. "You're dry. Go comb yourself out, you look like Medusa with a head full of snakes."

"What are you going to do, baby?"

"I have to make a phone call. It's kind of confidential, so I'd appreciate it if you—both of you—would go into the other room and close the door."

Moira got up and turned to look at me searchingly. "I said you were a government man. I'll bet you're calling Washington."

She was perfectly right, of course. She usually was. I said, "Go comb your golden tresses like a good girl."

She studied me for a moment longer. Then she moved her shoulders minutely, dismissing whatever it was that had bothered her. I wished I could dismiss what was bothering me so easily.

"The gadget you want is over there," she said. "There are no extensions. Come on, Mrs. Logan, he wants privacy."

I watched them go out of the room together, Beth slender and ladylike and half a head taller. The kid looked small and bouncy beside her. I went to the phone and called the regular Washington number and went through the routine formalities. Then I had Mac on the line. One thing about the guy, he may be a tricky bastard to work for, but he's never off playing golf when you need him.

"Eric here," I said. "I thought you'd like to hear about my vacation, sir."

Mac's voice was dry. "Are you having a wonderful time, Eric? Do you wish I were there—so you could punch my nose?"

"You might have told me my family was involved."

"It seemed better to let you discover it for yourself," he said. "You might have had some inconvenient scruples about visiting them as an agent on official business; you might have felt I was asking you to spy on them."

"Weren't you?"

He laughed and ignored the question. His voice became more businesslike: "I'm acquainted with developments up to Paul's last report. I also have a medical statement indicating that Paul's injuries were more purposeful than malicious, if you know what I mean. Not that there weren't indications of gratuitous violence, but on the whole it appears that Paul's assailant had a definite aim in mind." Mac cleared his throat. "Did he talk?"

"Paul?" I said. "It would seem so."

"Your evidence?"

"Martell knows all about me, even to my code name. Of course, he might have learned it elsewhere, but considering the short time I've been back in the service, it seems unlikely." After a moment, guessing what was in Mac's mind, I said, "Anybody can be made to talk, sir."

"True, with reservations. But I wasn't criticizing Paul, only myself for putting him in that position. I . . . shouldn't have sent him ahead to operate alone, Eric. I knew he wasn't up to it, not against a man like Martell. I . . ." There was a little silence. I was a little embarrassed. I mean, you don't want a guy like Mac to turn human on you. It shakes your faith in immutable things like life and death and the movements of the heavenly bodies. I heard him clear his throat again; then he said crisply: "Martell must have taken some action on his information, or you wouldn't know he had it."

"Yes, sir. He tried to get his boss, Fredericks, to dispose of me, at least temporarily. I'm assuming the inspiration came from Martell. He's handicapped to some extent by the fact that he has to maintain his cover as an obedient goon. Fredericks would start asking pointed questions if he caught his hired hand operating independently." After a moment, I said, "Question, sir."

"Yes?"

"We seem to be assuming that Martell's on some mysterious mission in this country, and has been on it for seven years or more. Has anybody considered the possibility that he might be on the up-and-up, in a crooked sort of way?"

"What do you mean, Eric?"

"Well, he could have chased after just one woman too many. Suppose he just got himself kicked off the team. He had to earn a living somehow, poor fellow, so he came over here and got a job carrying a gun for an American racketeer, since that was the kind of work he knew best. When Rizzi went to jail, he simply scouted the employment market and hooked up with the man paying top wages, who happened to be Fredericks."

"On this basis, how do you explain what happened to Paul?"

"Easily, sir. Naturally Martell doesn't want guys like Paul and me snooping around—not because he's conducting some secret operation for the other side, but simply because we threaten his new identity as Jack Fenn. Just like a crook who's gone straight for years wouldn't want a detective with a long memory threatening his new-found respectability."

"Do you believe this, Eric?"

"I don't believe or disbelieve. I just think it's a possibility that ought to be considered."

"It has been," Mac said, "and dismissed from consideration."

"Why?"

"For one thing, the people he worked for, as you must

know, have a very permanent way of discharging employees who prove unsatisfactory. Very few of them turn up in the labor market afterwards. But you are right to a certain extent. We've learned that Martell did get himself into disgrace again, presumably some time between fifty-one, when we know he was working for them in Berlin, and fifty-three, when he first came into contact with our police under the name of Fenn."

"How did you learn this, sir?"

"With Martell, how would we learn it except from one of his castoff women. Fortunately, she had a grudge, and we worked on it and got what she knows. Although he's not ordinarily a heavy drinker, he apparently did talk in his cups on a couple of occasions. He felt somebody had given him a raw deal, she said. 'Just one little slip and they send you to Siberia!' was the way he put it —America being Siberia, in his estimation. He tried to impress her with what a big man he'd been somewhere else, and what a come-down it was for him to be running errands for a punk like Rizzi."

I said, when he paused, "That still doesn't prove—"

"There's more," Mac said. "The girl was scared at hearing him talk that way about a big shot like Rizzi, and showed it. Martell laughed at her and said something about how Rizzi might think he, Martell, Fenn as she knew him, was running Rizzi's errands, but actually it was the other way around. . . . When he sobered up, he beat her up and almost killed her. He said he would kill her if she repeated anything he'd said."

"Martell being what he is, I have no doubt he meant it."

"Neither had she," Mac said. "But the two thousand odd miles between New York and Reno apparently made her feel safe enough, after he'd gone west to join Fredericks recently, to start brooding over her wrongs in various bars, more or less aloud, and somebody picked it up and passed it to us."

I said, "Well, that does put a different light on it. So Martell felt he was using Rizzi in some way. That's interesting."

"Very." After a moment, Mac went on: "I've studied the interrogation tapes carefully, Eric. Reading between the lines, so to speak—there's more that I won't bother to quote—I've come to the conclusion that Mr. Martell's 'one little slip,' actually his third on record, of course, came very close to getting him liquidated. He was saved —I'm guessing now—because somebody needed a man who could do a good job of impersonating a tough American gangster. Just an ordinary intelligence agent wouldn't do. The man had to be tough enough, and skilled enough with weapons, to maneuver himself into the position of being the trusted lieutenant of a big-shot like Rizzi. So Martell was reprieved, but he was reprimanded, demoted, and sent over here to ponder his sins and spend seven years building a reputation and a police record—for what?"

"Yes," I said. "It's a good question. And from Rizzi, he moves to Fredericks. What's the common denominator, sir, if there is one?"

"There is one," Mac said.

"Yes," I said. "Dope."

"Precisely."

I hesitated, and said, "A friend of mine had an experience on the Mexican border that may fit in with all this. Returning to her native land, she had her car searched very thoroughly, which had never happened before. She has the theory that it was because she happens to be Sally Fredericks' daughter."

Mac's voice was dry. "You have a valuable knack of making interesting and useful friends, Eric."

I ignored the interruption. "She also has the theory that her male parent might be trying to get something across the border, and that she was suspected of carrying it for him. Confirm or deny, sir."

"Your friend is a fast girl with a theory. Confirm." Mac was silent briefly, then he asked, "What do you know about heroin, Eric?"

"That it's habit-forming, sir. What's going on? Are they sending guys like Martell to turn us into a nation of hop-heads so they can take us over easier? Like the

British are supposed to have encouraged the opium trade in the last century to make the Chinese more tractable?"

"It's a possibility," Mac said. "But it does seem a little far-fetched."

"To go back to my friend's experience," I said. "Could Fredericks perhaps be having difficulties getting the stuff across the border these days?"

"He could."

"Serious difficulties, like having his lines of communications disrupted by crude individuals wearing badges? Serious enough that somebody'd think he was desperate enough to try using his own daughter as a courier?"

"Something like that."

"A large shipment, perhaps?"

"Quite large. It was traced from Italy to Mexico and the border was warned that it was moving north. Twice it was almost seized when The Man, as he is known, tried to bring it in through his normal channels. Various small fish were caught, but the bait was not taken with them. Rumors are that The Man made a serious error at this point."

"Such as?"

"Such as enlisting local help, which proved unreliable and greedy. You can't call it an actual hijacking, since the gentlemen below the border are quite amenable to reason, as long as it's a large enough reason in American dollars. The Man, to date, has refused to pay, although there's evidence that his supplies are getting low and his distributors are beginning to complain. Instead he sent a trusted expert south to deal with the problem, but the individual apparently wasn't quite expert enough, and disappeared. I have most of this information from another agency, which is giving us full cooperation."

"How full?" I asked. "If I fall over a guy in the dark, can I kick him hard, or is he apt to be one of Mr. Anslinger's nice young men?"

"We have a clear field," Mac said. "Up to a point. Understandably, they don't want the shipment to get loose in the country. Understandably, too, they would like very much to get something concrete and legal on

Mr. Salvatore Frederici, alias Fredericks. But I have persuaded them, by lying shamefully, that we know exactly what we're doing, and that our mission must have priority, in the national interest. I'd hate to have to eat my words, Eric."

"Yes, sir," I said. "Just what the hell are we doing?"

"We are finding out what Martell is up to," Mac said. "Disgraced or not, they wouldn't waste a man of his caliber on something completely unimportant. Actually, you'll also be acting in behalf of your family, Eric. I think you can see that anything that clarifies our problem is in their best interest, particularly if you can manage to give our cooperative associates the evidence they need against Fredericks. Judging by the reports I have here, the situation of Mr. Logan and his dependents should be a great deal more peaceful with Fredericks out of the way."

"You don't have to sell me the job, sir," I said, rather stiffly. "Anyway, I'm hardly staying up nights worrying about Logan's situation, and I doubt that you are. Beth and the kids are another matter, of course, as far as I'm concerned. Am I authorized to take steps to protect them, if necessary?"

"If necessary," Mac said. "But remember, your mission is not to protect your family, or even to get the goods on Mr. Fredericks, desirable though that might be. Your immediate responsibility is to discover Martell's mission—"

"What do our cooperative friends think about it?"

"They have no theories. It came as a surprise to them that he was anything but what he seemed. Their feeling is that he was hired as a replacement for the trusted gentleman who went to Mexico and wasn't expert enough to return."

"Contradiction, sir."

"You have evidence to the contrary?"

"Not evidence, just a hunch. Martell is a replacement, all right, but I doubt that he's in line to go to Mexico. He's too new and I don't have the feeling that Fredericks trusts him very far—not a thousand miles and a good many thousand dollars, I wouldn't think. There's a man Sally trusts a good deal more."

"Logan?"

"Yes, sir. In my opinion, Martell—or Fenn—is just an insurance policy Fredericks took out so he wouldn't get his head blown off when he started putting pressure on Logan. After all, he'd just lost his previous number one, from what you say, south of the border. And that's kind of interesting, when you come to think about it."

"What do you mean?"

I said, "Martell needs a job. Fredericks' most trusted man disappears, creating a vacancy. Do you think there might be a connection?"

"The thought had occurred to me," Mac said. "The possibility is being investigated."

"Anyway," I said, "Fredericks hired Martell, or Fenn, to guard the body; but I have a strong feeling the man he wants for the Mexico jaunt is the Duke."

"Your reasons?"

"It just adds up, that's all. Why else would he be scaring women and children out at the ranch? I'll check with Beth, but I think I'm right."

"It seems like an odd selection. A man with whom he's quarreled, according to my information; a man who has good reason to hate him?"

I said, "Ah, but you don't understand these gentleman adventurers like Mr. Logan. He's a man of principle, he draws lines. He's that rarity these days, a man of his word. Regardless of personalities, if the Duke says he's going to Mexico and coming back, he's going to Mexico and coming báck, and Fredericks knows it. All he has to do is get the Duke to say it."

"This Logan sounds like an interesting person," Mac said.

"Yes, sir," I said. "Interesting. Did you get another man out here?"

"Yes."

"Will you send him an alert signal immediately. A safe place for something I want to put in storage temporarily and someone to watch over it. I'll check with him in twenty minutes."

"I think it can be arranged." He gave me a number to call. "Eric."

"Yes?"

"After you learn Martell's mission, you can remember the standing orders for people in his category. They should be carried out, however, with at least a semblance of legality, to keep our brother agencies happy. Keep this in mind, particularly if you should have to deal with Fredericks as well."

I said, "I'd feel silly as hell trying to make an arrest."

Mac said calmly, "Unfortunately, your feelings are a matter of complete unconcern to the government you serve."

"Well, I always suspected it," I said, "but it's nice to have it in the form of an official statement. . . . Oh, I almost forgot. A detail."

"Proceed."

"Two unsavory characters just entered, illegally, a residence at the following Reno address." I gave the address. "They were attacked and killed by a dog belonging to the mistress of the house, not present. The dog was badly injured and had to be destroyed by the first person to discover the gory spectacle. Police are trying to contact the animal's owner, currently without success. Can you fix?"

"I think so. I gather you want publicity."

"Yes, sir. Particularly the fact that the lady of the house is missing. Radio and TV if possible. And the guy who's going to destroy the dog had better be warned that it's already dead."

"I see," Mac said softly. "I love your details, Eric."

"Yes," I said. "They're nice, aren't they? Good-bye, sir."

Chapter Seventeen

       I KNOCKED on the bedroom door. Beth came out. Behind her, I caught a glimpse of the kid working on herself with comb and brush, in front of the dresser mirror.

"Whom were you calling, Matt?" Beth asked.

"My boss. You met him," I said.

"Oh, the gray-haired man who came out last year and tried to persuade me not to—"

"Yes."

"He wasn't very diplomatic. Everything he told me about . . . about your work was, well, shocking, to say the least."

"Sure." I found myself wondering just how hard Mac had actually tried to prevent the divorce. After all, reliable help is hard to get these days, and the work isn't suited to a married man with responsibilities.

Beth looked down at her hands, and said in a quite different tone, "I think you know what it's all about, don't you, Matt?"

"What Fredericks wants of the Duke? It wasn't too hard to guess, knowing Fredericks' current business and the Duke's former status and certain other things."

She said, "It was put as a straight business proposition first. Larry was to get a generous percentage for his trouble. Fredericks said he didn't mind paying one of his own men; he was just damned if he was going to be blackmailed by a bunch of . . . of lousy Greasers. If he did, he said, he'd never get a shipment through again without paying off to some bandit in a big hat. What he wanted was for somebody to go down there and scare the . . . put the fear of God into them." She studied her hands as if she'd never seen them before. "Larry refused, of course. He's not doing anything like that any more;

110

hasn't been for years. Besides, he says there's nothing as dirty as . . . as dope."

"Very high-principled of him, I'm sure."

She looked up angrily. "Do you have to keep jeering at him?"

"You don't really expect us to be bosom pals, do you?"

She sighed and looked down again. Obviously she thought it would be nice if we'd be bosom pals, or at least pretend to be, in a civilized manner.

She said, "Then the threats began. And the . . . incidents. There'd be riders in the hills who didn't belong there. Betsy would wander off for a moment and come back with a lollipop somebody'd given her, although we'd seen nobody around. The boys would go off on horseback, and a couple of agreeable strangers would show them a fascinating trail they'd never seen before. They'd come back quite safe, excited and pleased, but the meaning was clear. It's been . . . just a nightmare, for weeks."

"Sure," I said. "Well, we'll see if we can't put a stop to it. You go back to the Duke and . . . what did you say?" She hesitated, and shook her head. I went on: "I want both of you to go back to the ranch and sit tight. Tell the Duke I've got a proposition for him that I think will solve everybody's problems. Tell him I don't think there'll be any immediate trouble, but it would be just as well if he saw his way clear to passing up his afternoon nap, just this once."

"He doesn't take—" She checked herself, flushed, and said mildly, "He's only forty-six, Matt."

"That makes him about as much older than you are as I'm older than the kid in there," I said. "Interesting thought, isn't it? Anyway, tell him to keep his eyes open until I get there. Tell them I hate to intrude on his hospitality after being so politely shown the gate, but I think it's about time we joined forces. Where are the kids?"

"Peter took them to a friend's hunting lodge back in

the mountains. Clara's with them—the maid—and our three regular ranch hands. They have guns and know how to shoot. The place can only be reached if you have four-wheel drive or horses. Peter took the Land Rover."

"Well, the opposition apparently has horses available, from what you've said. It's either very good or very bad. If your men are alert, it could be a tough nut to crack, but if anything does happen, you won't know it for hours or even days, since I don't suppose there's a phone up there."

"Peter is to report in every morning at a definite hour." She hesitated. "Larry decided on it last night. He sent them all off early this morning."

"Well, that should give us enough time. Fredericks' real tough boys are probably from the city. This is a little different from riding around in the hills scaring women and children. Even if he knows the place, it'll take him a little while to mount an efficient wilderness operation for this kind of business."

"That's what Larry had in mind."

I said, "I think I've got it fixed for that mess in there to be cleaned up with no trouble to anybody."

She licked her lips. "I . . . we're very grateful. It was a dreadful mistake—"

"You can save your gratitude. I wouldn't lift a finger to keep the Duke out of trouble—particularly on a stunt like this—and I don't suppose his record can stand many more contacts with the law, even if he is a respectable rancher these days. But it just happened I wanted the news to go on the air that way, so he gets by with it again." I looked at her for a moment longer. Her color had come back, and she was really quite a nice-looking girl—well, I'd been of that opinion for years. I said, "Well, give my regards to Bwana Simba."

"To whom?"

"Bwana Simba? Oh, that's just what us old Africa hands call the great white hunter, a term of respect, don't you know? I think it means Master Lion, or some similar corn."

"You're being rather childish, aren't you, Matt?"

"Oh, rawther," I said. "Don't begrudge me a few such moments. I'm going to have to grow up fast now. On your way, Mrs. Logan. . . ."

When I came into the bedroom, the kid was well along towards having her hair up. Smooth and bright and neat and adult, it made an interesting contrast with her bare legs and gaudy blue shorts.

She spoke without turning her head. "Who's Eric, baby?"

I glanced towards the phone in the other room. "Some folks have big ears."

"I wasn't eavesdropping. But Fenn called you Eric, in Dad's office, and I've been wondering ever since. . . ." After a moment, she said, "It's a code name, isn't it?"

"Yes," I said, "it's a code name."

"Your code name."

"That's right. My code name. And when I'm Eric, let me tell you, I'm a real bastard."

She grinned at me impishly in the mirror. "You mean, I'll be able to tell the difference?"   ,

But it wasn't the way it had been, and we both knew it. Two people can go off together for a little while, sometimes, and find a secret time and place of their own, but the world is always waiting for them to come back. We were back.

I said, "Throw some stuff into a suitcase. You're moving out of here. Somebody else might have the same bright idea as the Duke, and there's always some danger when a big criminal organization breaks up."

She turned to look at me. "I see. You're moving in on Dad."

"Let's just say I'm moving." After a moment, I said, "I want you safe, kid."

She regarded me steadily for a little longer; then she shrugged her shoulders abruptly. "Okay, if you put it like that. . . ."

Five minutes later, we were out of there. It was a risk stopping by the motel, but I wanted the little .38 and some cartridges, as well as a clean shirt. Nothing happened and nobody followed us away.

I made sure of that; then I had her pull up for gas at a filling station. While the attendant was working on the Mercedes, I went over and used the pay phone on the wall. Mac had been on the job. The voice at the other end gave me directions, and said somebody would be there when we arrived. I gave some instructions in return.

When I came back to the car, Moira was sitting in the seat I'd been occupying.

"I thought maybe you'd like to drive it," she said. "It's a little different from that truck of yours. You can give it a real workout if you like. I've got three thousand miles on it; it's all broken in." She waited until I was sitting beside her, and went on, "That's the starter, over there. It's a four-speed shift, all-synchro, and reverse is over—"

I started it up, dropped it into reverse, backed out to clear a car being serviced ahead, and sent the little machine forward, picking up speed through the gears.

"Nuts," the kid said, "you've driven one before. I thought I was giving you a treat."

"Any Mercedes is a treat," I said.

"I heard you talking to Mrs. Logan," she said. "It sounds as if Dad's been giving them a rough time."

"He's a good strategist," I said. "He can see the enemy's weak points clearly. I mean, normally you don't go threatening a man like Duke Logan about his kids, no matter how retired he is. Because what happens is, you get a phone call one night and a gentle British voice says, *I say, old chap, if anything should happen to Peter, I'd have to hold you personally responsible, don't you know?* It's the natural reaction of anybody trained a certain way. It's what I'd do, and it's what Logan did, I'm sure."

"You sound . . . you sound as if you and the Duke had a lot in common. Besides a wife."

"Oh, we do," I said. "And don't forget Fenn. He's

one of the smoky boys, too, and a good one. . . .
But what I was saying is, Fredericks would know the
Duke meant every word of it. Your dad's goons could
ride around the hills looking menacing all they wanted
to; but the minute they made a real move, your dad
would know the Duke wouldn't spend one fraction of a
second over the boy. He'd leave that to his crew. Himself, he'd just wind up that fancy Jag of his and head
for town with a gun under his arm, and he wouldn't be
bluffing one little bit. No, your dad never had a chance
of pressuring Logan as long as there was just the boy."

"But I don't see how his getting married changed—"

I said, "The trouble with Logan's countermove, kid, is
that like the hydrogen bomb, it's a great deterrent, but
when it comes to actual use, it's more or less a one-shot
proposition. You can't go charging into town with blood
in your eye every time some mysterious stranger hands
a baby a lollipop. You've just got to sit out these harass-
ing tactics. Well, the Duke could do it, and his boy
probably just thought it was real exciting, like the mov-
ies, and my kids are too young to worry about things
like that. But Beth isn't what you'd call a real good
sitting-it-out type. She's led a sheltered, civilized life until
quite recently; her nerves aren't up to this kind of cold
warfare. So Fredericks twists the screws, bit by bit, never
really stepping over the line far enough to send the Duke
on the warpath—but meanwhile the lady of the ranch is
slowly going out of her mind with worry, and probably
not keeping it a secret from her embattled husband. He
can laugh at Fredericks, but if he loves her he can't
very well laugh at her."

Moira said, "That makes Dad a real creep, doesn't it?
Hitting at a man through a woman."

"Yes," I said, "it sure does."

She glanced at me quickly. Apparently there had been
something odd in my voice, of which I hadn't been aware.
I dropped the little Mercedes down a gear with a neat
job of double-clutching, and sent it charging up the
next hill with the tachometer riding the red danger-line.

It wasn't the hottest job in the world, but it smoothed out those Nevada back roads in a startling fashion, and stuck like glue in the curves.

The place was well back in the hills. We reached it after following a dirt track and a single telephone wire for a good many miles. It was a small ranch, complete with barns and corrals, but there didn't seem to be any people or livestock around. We pulled up in the dusty yard, and Moira laughed and pulled off the kerchief she'd put on to protect her hair, breathing deeply.

"All right," she said. "I'm convinced. You've driven one before. Let me order seatbelts before the next demonstration, please."

I waited without speaking, with my hand on the gun in my pocket. The front door opened and a youngish man came out. He gave me a certain signal, and I took my hand out of my pocket. I reached back and lifted Moira's suitcase out of the space behind the seats, and helped her out.

As we walked towards the house together, she said, "God, what a dead-looking joint. I hope I won't have to stay here long."

I didn't answer. The man who had greeted us, following my earlier instructions, was at the phone when we came in. I closed the door and put the suitcase down. The man signaled that he had the connection. I turned to look at the kid.

"I made you a promise once," I said.

"A promise?"

"I said that even if the situation should arise, I wouldn't ask you for help." She remembered, and her expression changed, becoming faintly puzzled and wary. I said, "Your dad is coming on the line. He's already a bit worried because of the radio reports saying you're missing. I'm going to talk to him now. I'm not asking you, Moira, I'm telling you: at a certain point in the conversation, you're going to scream. It will be a good, loud, scream. It will convince him I mean business, which I do. You won't be betraying him voluntarily. You'll be

screaming simply because you have to. You can remember that, later."

She took a step backwards, her eyes wide and shocked
and incredulous. Then I had a painful grip on her arm,
and the young man was beckoning me towards the
phone, urgently. . . .

Chapter Eighteen

I DROVE away from there fast, taking the little Merc. If it were seen in my possession later, so much the better. It would let Fredericks know I hadn't been bluffing when I said I was holding its owner hostage for his good behavior in certain specified regards.

It took me two hours to find my way by back roads to the Double-L Ranch. When I got there, it was approaching the same time of afternoon as when I'd seen it previously, and the place looked about the same, except that there didn't seem to be anybody around. Beth's Buick station wagon was parked in front of the door, however, headed out. I pulled up behind it, making the swing in the yard very smartly with a quick down-shift and some fine sports-car exhaust noises. It's a subdued and polite little car, not one of your raging beasts, but you can make it snarl a bit if you try.

I switched off and got out, stretching my legs and looking as casual as I could with all my senses tuned for trouble. Then the front door slammed open and Beth ran out of the house looking very breathless. She came to a sudden stop, staring at me in a surprised way.

"Matt!" she said. "Oh! I thought . . ." She checked herself abruptly.

I didn't get it at once. But she was looking so confused and guilty there had to be a reason, and I looked around and glanced at the Merc and recalled the youthful, noisy flourish with which I'd announced my arrival. I looked over towards the carport. The Land Rover was missing. Well, young Peter Logan had taken that to transport the kids and their retinue back into the mountains. But the big green Jaguar roadster was missing, too.

Nobody who's consciously compared the two would ever mistake the polite burble of the little Mercedes for

118

the roar of an XK-150S, but Beth hardly qualified as a sports-car expert. To her, a car was just something that ran until it stopped running, after which you got a man to fix it for you. I looked at her standing there, still in her lady-of-the-ranch costume, regarding the toes of her handsome saddle-leather pumps with downcast eyes, like a teen-ager in the principal's office.

"Where is he?" I asked.

She said, "Matt, I—"

I wanted to shake her. "Where's he gone?" I demanded. She didn't answer. I said, "Wherever it is, you obviously didn't expect him back so soon. Where'd you send him, Beth?"

She licked her lips. "I didn't . . ." She stopped. "It was just a . . . a stupid quarrel. . . ." She stopped again. "I couldn't stop him!" she breathed.

"He went to town after Fredericks? The damn fool! What does he think this is, a Wild West movie? I told you to sit tight, both of you!"

She said breathlessly, "No, you're wrong! That isn't where . . ." She was silent again.

I studied her face for a moment. "I see. At least I think I see. Where's a phone?"

She gave me a brief glance, turned, and fled into the house. I followed her and picked up the instrument in the hall to which she led me, got long distance, and went through the usual silly routine with her standing right there. To hell with security. They could change the damn code words tomorrow. They probably would, anyway. Then I had Mac on the wire again.

"Eric here," I said.

"Where have you been? We've been trying to reach you."

"I'm reached. Shoot."

Mac said, "I have here a report to the effect that Lawrence alias Duke Logan is aimed approximately south by southeast in a green Jaguar roadster license number YU 2-1774. An Arizona state police cruiser, alerted by a patrol farther north that saw him pass, tried to run him down but barely got close enough to confirm the number. I have the verbatim report of one of the officers here, to wit: *Jeez, if that guy fires the third stage he'll be in orbit.* Apparently they were doing well over a hundred and twenty when he pulled away from them. Comment?"

I looked at Beth, and suddenly I knew exactly how it had been. *A stupid quarrel,* she'd said. She was a hard girl to quarrel with, in the pots-and-pans-slinging sense, but that didn't mean she didn't have the ability to make a man so furious that he could hardly see. I'd lived with her; I knew her pretty well. I'd only met Logan once, but I knew him pretty well, too. He was the kind of man I understand easily.

"I think the newlyweds have had a spat, sir," I said into the phone, and I saw Beth cringe at the corny description. I went on: "If I'm correct, he's right on the ragged edge: he's driving sad and he's driving mad. When those cool, calm characters flip, they really flip. He's stomped out of the house, I figure, on an errand he doesn't care much for, and he's probably kind of hoping, subconsciously, that somebody'll arrest him before he has to go through with it, or that the Jag will flame out on him, or that he'll manage to kill himself, or something. But he'll be damned and blasted, old chap, if he'll stop of his own accord; and if he gets where he's going it'll be rawther tough, don't you know, on anybody who happens to get in his way. It should be something to see, if you've got a strong stomach."

Beth's eyes looked big and wounded. Mac's voice spoke in my ear: "The state police were considering a roadblock, but other agencies got wind of the situation and took a hand. At present he's merely being tracked, like a guided missile, but he'll be at the border presently. Advice has been requested, urgently."

I hesitated, and said, "They're damn fools if they stop him on the way down."

"That's the consensus here. And returning? Assuming that he does return? The previous man didn't, you remember."

I said, "My money's on the Duke. If that bomb he's

driving doesn't kill him, in his present mood, no two-bit Mexican desperado will."

"And your advice?"

"It depends on whether they want some kilos of the white stuff or a guy named Sally."

Mac said, "That's all very well for them, Eric, but you're not forgetting that it isn't Fredericks we're after?"

"I'm not forgetting," I said. "But I don't relish the thought of trying to make a man like Martell talk by direct methods, even assuming I could get him alone, in a suitable place, alive, which is a lot of assuming. If he was using Rizzi, the chances are he's using Fredericks the same way. So let's take Fredericks out from under him and see what happens."

"If they let him come back through, with cargo, can you guarantee safe delivery eventually? It's a big shipment, and they don't want to take chances on its getting loose in the country."

I said, "Sir, do you want me to hang up on you?"

"Eric—"

"Guarantee! What kind of jackass talk is that, with all due apologies?"

He sighed, two thousand odd miles away. "I know. I was instructed to ask."

I said, "So there's a risk, and maybe everything will go wrong, and there'll be many happy dreams sold at a thousand per cent profit. All I can say is that if they stop Duke Logan with cargo, all they'll get is Duke Logan with cargo. If they let him through, there are intriguing possibilities, but the word is possibilities."

"You have a plan in mind?"

"How can I have? The Duke took off before I could talk him into doing for us what he's now doing on his own accord. I haven't had a chance to talk with him at all. I'm going to have to intercept him somehow, before he makes delivery at this end, and it's going to be tough, since I don't know anything about his arrangements. But he must have made some or he wouldn't know where to go, down there, or where to come, up here. . . . Wait a minute."

I was still watching Beth. Her expression had changed slightly. She said quickly, "I know . . . something that may help. I heard him talking on the phone."

I nodded, and spoke to Mac: "We apparently have a lead of sorts. We'll see what can be done, if he gets back."

Mac said, "I'll see what I can do at this end. The rest is kind of up to Mr. Logan, don't you know?"

"Righto, sir."

There's something about that clipped, British—or phony-British—way of talking that's terribly contagious, don't you know?

Chapter Nineteen

I PUT THE phone down. I was looking at Beth, but for some reason I was seeing a long, low, green car—the color is known as British Racing Green—hurtling across the Arizona desert with that fine, wicked sound that you get only from high-class machinery that's really carrying the mail. Barring the true racing cars, the Jaguar is possibly, along with its American counterpart the Corvette, the most ridiculous vehicle made, from the viewpoint of efficient and economical transportation. You've got power enough to move a ten-ton truck attached to a loadspace barely adequate for two men and a small toothbrush. But it's an ego-satisfying machine in every respect; and I kind of wished I was down there, flying co-pilot with the Duke. I've done some fast driving myself, from time to time.

Well, he'd just have to make it on his own. Sooner or later, most men do. I looked at Beth.

"What did you say to him?" I asked. "Something silly like, 'If anything happens to the children I'll never forgive you'?"

She said quickly, "I didn't mean—"

"No, of course not."

"I never asked him to give in to Fredericks! You can't believe . . . I never dreamed he'd do it! I didn't want him to! I just—"

"You just went desperate on him," I said. "He'd done everything he could do—except that one thing. He'd made the kids as safe as he could. He'd even tried to get Moira Fredericks as a hostage. That was going pretty far, but you were pushing him hard, weren't you? And that plan fizzled, and you couldn't take it any more, and you started telling him how you'd feel if anything went wrong —as if he didn't already know—and it got to the point

123

where he'd had it. He just looked you in the eye and walked to the phone and said, *Logan here. You win. I'm ready to deal.*"

She started to speak, but changed her mind. I didn't have the words right, of course; he hadn't said exactly that, nor had she. But it had happened more or less that way, and they'd both glared at each other full of pride and resentment—they hadn't been married long enough to work out a way of handling these things. They'd both been adults for years, to be sure, but the marriage itself was very young.

He'd made his call, and she'd stood by, not believing he really meant it, and he'd stalked out to the four-wheeled projectile under the carport, not believing she'd really let him go. He'd switched it on, started it up, and sat there for a moment watching the gauges. You don't take off with a sports-car engine stone-cold, not even in the middle of a family explosion. She'd have thought happily that he was reconsidering; even so, she'd have been thinking of going out to him, just thinking it, when the Jag backed out sharply, swung around, and shot ahead.

Then she'd come running across the yard, no doubt, but he'd be watching the tach now and reaching for second gear, keeping the revs down because the mill was still cold, concentrating on the car because everything had gone too far and it was too late and he didn't even want to hear her calling after him, if she did call. . . .

"Please don't look at me like that!" Beth whispered. "Matt, what are we going to do?"

Suddenly I felt kind of sorry for her. I mean, I suppose a woman ought to be able to get a little frantic now and then without causing her man to do more than slam the door hard on his way out.

I said, "We'll figure something, but first, what's the chances of getting something to eat around here? I haven't had anything since breakfast, and the circumstances weren't favorable to good digestion, if you'll recall."

She hesitated; it was clearly hard for her to think of such mundane things as food. "There's cold roast," she said, "and I think there are some cold boiled potatoes. I could fry them for you. You used to like them fried, didn't you?"

It made me feel funny that she should remember that. "Yes," I said. "If you don't mind, I'll stop in the living room and make myself a drink. . . . Do you have a road atlas?"

"Yes, it's in the living room, too. On the shelf under the window."

A little later, she came into the living room with a tray of food and a small silver ice bucket. I looked up from the atlas, as she took some cubes from the bucket and dropped them into my warm drink.

"What are you looking for, Matt?"

"I was kind of figuring the earliest he could be back," I said. "According to my information, he's heading south southeast, which doesn't tell us much. I don't know the border very well, at least not from the dope-smuggler's angle. . . . When did he leave?"

She hesitated, and glanced at her watch. "It was . . . quite a while ago."

"It must have been," I said, "for him to be clear down in Arizona already. He must have that Jag really screaming. Well, let's hope he hangs onto it, or they'll be picking up pieces of Logan all over the southwest."

Her breath caught. "You don't have to say things like that, Matt!"

"Sorry," I said. I looked up at her. "How the hell *did* you come to marry him, anyway, Beth?"

"Can't you understand?" she said. "Can't you understand that I couldn't do it twice?"

"What do you mean?"

"I met him," she said. "I liked him very much. He liked me. I thought I knew what was coming when he asked me, very formally, to have dinner with him out here. I was right, of course. He said he wanted to . . . to ask me to marry him. But first, he said, there was something he had to tell me. . . . He told me. Everything."

"Stout fella," I said.

She paid me no attention. "I was shocked, of course,"

she said, "terribly shocked. He hadn't seemed like that sort of person at all, any more than you. . . . Matt, do you think I have an . . . an affinity for men who . . . do you think I really, subconsciously, under all my civilized ideas and ideals, want someone . . . someone violent . . . ?"

"You mean," I said, "like the prissy schoolmarm type really wants to be raped?"

She flushed, and went on quickly: "Anyway, Larry saw on my face what I was thinking. 'I'm sorry, my dear,' he said, 'it was too much to ask, of course.' And he had exactly the same weary look that you had when you said we might as well call it a day. And I couldn't do it again, don't you understand? I couldn't do it a second time! I know you think I failed you, and I still think you had no right to expect . . . But I couldn't do it to him, too. I just couldn't!" After a while, she said quietly, "Maybe it would have been better if I had. I . . . I'm not very good at this sort of thing, Matt." Presently she added, with a touch of defiance, "I don't think anyone should have to be!"

I said, "It would be nice if thinking made it so."

I frowned at her for a moment longer, wondering if there could have been some basis for her theory about herself; it *was* odd that twice she should have picked men with dark secrets. Well, her subconscious was her problem. I yawned and put the atlas aside and started to eat. The drink had been a mistake. It had only reminded me of all the hours I'd been without sleep. When Beth spoke again, her voice seemed to come from far away.

I asked, "What did you say?"

"What did you do with that sexy little girl? That's her car outside, isn't it?"

I wished she hadn't asked. I had a sudden picture of the kid as I'd last seen her. *I asked you what side you were on,* Moira had whispered, *and you kissed me. I asked you why we had to come here and you said because you wanted me safe. Safe!* I had no trouble at all remembering the contempt in her voice and expression.

I said, "I traded that sexy little girl for a safe-conduct

pass for the kids. When young Peter checks in tomorrow morning, tell him it's okay to bring them home."

Beth frowned. "I don't understand—"

I said, "I'm not too proud to borrow a good idea. There was nothing wrong with the Duke's plan except its execution. I just went ahead with it after you left."

"You mean—"

"I mean," I said, "she's being held in a certain place. Fredericks has been notified that anything that happens to my kids happens to his kid, too. I think I managed to convince him that I mean it." I drew a long breath. "In other words, we've got the children off the streets. We've canceled them out. It's just a game for grown-ups, now."

Beth was still frowning. Then her forehead cleared. "I see. Well, I don't suppose she's very proud of her parent, and she seemed quite fond of you; I suppose she was glad to cooperate—"

"I didn't ask her," I said.

Beth's frown was back. "But then, how did you manage—"

I said, "I twisted her arm until she screamed. It was a very convincing scream. Anyway, I think Fredericks bought it."

Beth was staring at me wide-eyed. "You can't be serious! Why, the child was obviously in love with you! She'd have done anything—"

"Love, shmove," I said. It was like being in a foreign country, speaking a language nobody understood. "Look," I said, "that sexy little girl, as you call her, has very odd, almost biblical notions about family. You know, honor thy father and mother, that sort of thing. Her father happens to be a racketeer and her mother's a hopeless alcoholic, but as far as she's concerned that's strictly beside the point, and so is the fact that she's not really very fond of the old man. He's her old man, and that's that. Now, what am I going to do, kiss her gently and ask her to save humanity by casting her lot with the forces of truth and beauty represented by myself? And then have her spend the rest of her life remembering—with the old man dead or in jail—that she had a hand in putting him there; that she let herself be sweet-talked into turning against him? Nuts. So now she has a sore arm for a couple of days instead of a sore conscience for the rest of eternity. And she hates me, but that's not going to do her any harm; probably she's better off for it."

Beth was still staring at me as if I'd sprouted claws and fangs. It didn't matter, apparently, what you did to people's psyches, but twisting their arms was terrible. Then she thought of something else, and her expression changed.

"But if you have the girl—if you're holding her—then everything is all right, isn't it? I mean, Larry doesn't have to . . . to go through with it. We can trade her for—"

"For what?" I asked. "Do you think Fredericks is going to walk into a police station and sign a notarized confession of his crimes just because I happen to be holding his daughter somewhere? Don't be silly. All I've done is buy our kids a kind of temporary immunity, and don't think Fredericks isn't doing his damnedest to figure a way to hit back. Holding Moira Fredericks doesn't solve a thing. It just gives us a little time in which to operate more freely than we could if we had to worry about what might be happening to Betsy and the boys . . ."

"What about Peter?" she asked quickly.

I shrugged. "What about Peter Logan? He's old enough to vote and he's no kid of mine."

She stared at me, shocked. "You mean you didn't—"

I drew a long breath. "It was a simple deal, Beth. It had to be drawn in simple terms that a guy like Fredericks could understand and believe. An eye for an eye, something of his for something of mine. If I'd tried to cover the whole world, he'd have known I was pulling a bluff on him. Peter's got a papa of his own; he's no responsibility of mine, and Fredericks knows it. Let the Duke worry about Peter. Okay?"

She said angrily, "No, it's not at all okay—"

"Well, that's the deal," I said. "It's better than nothing, isn't it? Now what about this clue that you picked up listening in on your husband's telephone conversation?"

She was still glaring at me. "I wasn't listening in—"

"All right, you weren't listening in, you were just listening. What did you hear?"

"Matt, really!"

I drew a long breath. "I'm sorry. I haven't been to bed for longer than I can remember—not to sleep, anyway—and I'm probably a little unreasonable. Now, having apologized, may I have the clue?"

She started to speak angrily, checked herself, and said, "It's the old Buckman cabin."

"What's the old Buckman cabin?"

"Where they're to meet afterwards. After Larry gets back."

"I see. And where's the old Buckman cabin?"

"About seventeen miles back down the road you came by, there's a little road that turns down into a canyon, Buckman Canyon. It goes on for miles, and meets the highway way out on the desert—"

"Show me on the map."

She showed me. I went to the window and looked out. There was still plenty of daylight left, but there wasn't anything left inside me. It hits you like that sometimes. I shouldn't have had that drink. I tried to think what should be done next, but my brain was made strictly from absorbent cotton of a very crude and unrefined grade. Well, fortunately there was time to do something about it. Even with the best luck in the world, Logan couldn't possibly be back until morning unless he took to the air, and I know these fast-car boys. Unless the wheels fall off, they'll stick to what they're driving, rather than entrust themselves to some crazy pilot and his dangerous flying machine.

I turned from the window. You mustn't ever show that you're so pooped you don't know what the hell you're doing. You must always act as if you had a wonderful plan and it was working out swell. Anyway, that's the theory.

I went to the gun rack on the wall. Logan had an

adequate, but not spectacular, hunting arsenal. There was a handsome, light, double-barreled shotgun, 16-gauge, obviously of English make. There was an American 12-gauge with a long 30-inch barrel, a long-range weapon for ducks and geese that the little gun wouldn't reach. There was a bolt-action Winchester .270 with a scope, a nice, flat-shooting mountain rifle. And then, so help me, there was the Africa gun, the big double rifle, the .500 elephant buster, without which no real white hunter could stay in business. So he'd actually been there and done it. I made a silent apology to Mr. Lawrence Logan, wherever he might be and whatever speed he might be traveling at.

I took down the little 16-gauge double. There were shells in the ammunition drawer. I stuck one into each chamber after checking that the bores were clear. I closed the gun and took it to Beth.

"This is the safety," I said. "Shove it up so and you're ready to go. I'm going to have to ask you to baby-sit me for a while. Fredericks or Fenn may dream up something fancy and there's no use taking chances. I'm going to get some sleep on the sofa so I'll be ready to function when it's time for the Duke to get back. When's daylight around here?"

She hesitated. "I think it starts to get light about four. But—"

"Wake me at three, if I'm still out," I said. "Now, I want you to listen closely. You'll stay in this room with me, and you'll keep the gun in your hands, or in your lap, if you want to sit and read. Aim it some direction where it won't do too much damage if it goes off. If you hear anything—anything whatever—push off the safety with your thumb and put your finger on the trigger, like this. Either trigger, but it's customary to start with the rear. If you have the slightest real intimation of trouble, just pull the trigger."

"But—"

"Beth," I said, "please! I know it's a little rough on the household furnishings, but we hope you won't have to do it. But if you should, just follow instructions, do you understand? Don't scream, don't wait to turn around and see what's behind you, and don't for the love of Pete go out of the room to investigate. Just blow a hole in the wall. If anybody's trying to rush you, the noise should make him hit the deck. It should give me time to wake up and get into action. And if you should have to leave the room for any reason whatever, wake me up. Got it?"

"I . . . I think so. Matt."

"Yes?"

"What about . . ." She touched her lips with her tongue. "What about Larry?"

"What do you mean?"

"What will happen to him? The police don't like him or trust him. Even now, after all the years he's been here, if anything happens in Reno—in Fredericks' organization. . . They would come out here to harass him—"

"He should have retired a little farther away."

She said, "If you know Larry at all, you know he wouldn't do that. If he was going to live it down, he was going to live it down right here. He wasn't going to run off and hide somewhere. . . . What'll happen to him, Matt? They've just been waiting for him to get into trouble so they could—"

I said, "He's in trouble. He's smuggling heroin across the border in large quantities, which is illegal." I looked at her sharply. "You're really fond of the guy, aren't you?"

She said, "He's a wonderful person. And it was my fault . . . if it hadn't been for me . . ." She drew a long breath. "I . . . I'll do *anything* to help—"

She stopped. I looked down at her for a moment, and she started blushing. I grinned. "Make me the same offer some time when I'm not so sleepy." I took her chin in my hand, and tipped her face up, and kissed her on the lips in a brotherly fashion. "Don't worry too much about it, Beth. We usually take care of people who give us a hand, personal differences to the contrary notwithstanding."

I went over to the sofa, arranged the .38 revolver in a suitable location, and found a pillow of reasonable size. I kicked off my shoes, lay down, and went to sleep immediately.

When I woke up, Martell was there.

Chapter Twenty

IT WAS THE phone that woke me. I heard it ringing miles away, and I wished somebody'd silence it and let me sleep. Then I was suddenly wide awake wondering where she was and why she didn't do something about it. I started reaching for the little Smith and Wesson very cautiously. The gun wasn't there.

"Take it nice and easy, Buster," a man's voice said. I recognized the voice, although I'd heard it only once before, in Fredericks' office.

I opened my eyes, and there he was, sitting in a big chair facing the sofa with an automatic pistol balanced on his knee. It was a foreign job I didn't recognize; you can't keep track of them all these days. It had the usual switches and levers in the usual places. I judged the caliber to be about .38 inches or 9 mm.

Beth was sitting on the arm of the chair, very still. His left arm was around her, holding her there, and his left hand was where you'd expect the hand of a guy like that to be in a situation like that. Even if he'd had no interest in such things as Martell—and the record showed otherwise—he had to live up to his character as Fenn, and they're all breast-happy, those rackets boys. Maybe their mothers switched them to the bottle too early—if they had mothers.

The English shotgun, I noticed, had been carefully returned to its place on the rack. The two shells it had contained stood, base-down, on a nearby table, to let me know the piece was unloaded and there was no point in my building any fancy plans around it. He wasn't missing any bets. He was a pro.

"The knife," he said. "Careful now."

That's the trouble with showing your best tricks to punks like Tony and Ricky. When you really need them,

133

they're common knowledge. Well, he probably wouldn't have let me get away with it, anyway. I reached cautiously into my pocket and got out the Solingen knife with thumb and forefinger.

"Let it drop on the rug."

I did so.

"Go get it, Duchess." He released her. She stood up uncertainly. He gave her an encouraging pat on the rear. "Go on. Get it and bring it here, Duchess." He grinned. "Duchess. Duke-Duchess. Get it?"

The other man in the room laughed dutifully, bringing himself to my attention for the first time. He wasn't much, just a competent workman with a broken nose in a wide, cruel face. One look and I knew he knew nothing whatever. He'd be the reason Martell was still putting on his Fenn act for us—or maybe he'd just played the role so long it came natural to him now.

The other man said, "The phone, Fenn."

"What about the damn phone?"

"It's still ringing."

"I know," Martell said. "I realize it's painful as hell, Joey, but just try to bear up under the agony a few minutes longer, huh?" He gave Beth a shove. "Go on, Duchess. The knife. Get it."

Beth moved forward as awkwardly as if she were trying out her first pair of high heels. She stopped by the sofa and looked down at me.

"I . . . I'm sorry, Matt."

"Sure," I said.

There were no signs of a struggle. They'd just walked in, probably through the open study door near the fireplace—there was an outside door in the other room, I recalled—and taken the loaded gun from her before she could bring herself to shoot. I should have known that was what would happen, if the occasion should arise. I'd asked too much of her, although it hadn't seemed like much at the time.

She had that strange aversion to making a mess, or a loud noise—to making a fool of herself—that seems to afflict all respectable people. The idea of discharging a great big destructive firearm, or even a little one, in her own living room, perhaps for nothing, had seemed just too outlandish. She'd waited until she was absolutely sure it was necessary, and then, of course, it had been too late.

I couldn't help thinking of women I'd worked with who, given a shotgun and sufficient shells, could have guarded my sleep against an army of Martells and Joeys, but that wasn't fair. She wasn't Maria, or Tina, or any of those girls I'd known during the war, savage fighting animals, species human, gender feminine. She was Elizabeth Logan who had been Beth Helm, gentle wife and mother.

"I . . . I couldn't help it," she breathed.

"Sure."

Her lips formed a word, soundlessly. The word was, "Peter."

Behind her, Martell stirred impatiently. "Pick it up and bring it here!" he commanded.

She wasn't sure I'd got it. She signaled desperately with her eyes, indicating that there was someone or something outside, and spoke the name silently again as she bent to pick up the knife. She turned away and carried it to Martell. He looked at it and seemed surprised at its smallness, but made no comment. He dropped it into his own pocket.

"Get up," he said to me. I got up and put my feet into my shoes. "Okay," he said. "Now we'll take care of that damn phone and put Joey out of his misery. You get it, Duchess. If they ask what took you so long, say you were out. You just came in, the two of you, to hear the phone ringing. Find out who it is and what they want. One wrong word and you'll wish you hadn't. Got it? Now march."

There wasn't much chance yet, I told myself. He was still sizing me up, ready for trouble. There wasn't any hurry. If he'd wanted us dead immediately, he'd had plenty of opportunity to achieve his wish. He was saving us for something, so there was no need to risk the long, long gamble of taking action now, while he was alert and wary.

Besides, if the boy were actually outside, he might create a diversion. I remembered now that Beth had said he was to check in every morning at a certain hour. I wasn't counting too much on him, however. This wasn't a game for college kids in high-heeled boots.

"Fenn!" Joey said.

"What now?"

"The phone!"

"What about it?"

"It's stopped!"

Martell listened. "Well, damned if it hasn't," he said mildly. "Feel better now, Joey?"

They were both looking towards the hall door, as if waiting for the instrument to start ringing again. So were Beth and I. In that moment, there was a crash behind us, as the study door slammed back against the stone fireplace. A boy's voice commanded:

"Drop that gun! Put your hands up!"

If he'd shot one, as he should have, I'd have taken out the other for him. I was ready to hit Joey just as hard and dirty as I could. But I'd been right in not counting too much on young Mr. Logan. He was just a kid and he wanted to talk.

"Don't move! Hold it just like that!"

Beth turned, beside me. "Peter! Oh, thank God—"

It seemed to me she was offering up thanks a little prematurely. I let my breath go out very softly. There was a very bad taste in my mouth; I don't like amateur productions. I turned slowly.

He was there all right, in his cowboy boots and big hat, with his trusty thirty-thirty in his fists. He looked as if he'd just ridden Hiyo Silver off the range. It was disillusioning to realize that he'd undoubtedly arrived in an imported, four-wheel-drive Land Rover.

He must have spotted something wrong—a strange car in the yard, perhaps—and left his vehicle at a distance and come forward on foot to investigate. You've got to give him credit for that much, I suppose, but it would have been nice if his daddy had taught him what to do with that firearm he was brandishing.

He was still on the dialogue pitch, however. "Now, drop it like I said!" he snapped, aiming the rifle at Martell, who was, I saw, getting an amused, tolerant, and kind of pitying look on his face. He even glanced at me and shook his head almost imperceptibly, as one pro to another, asking me, I guess, to witness that it wasn't his fault if children attacked him and he had to defend himself.

Young Logan was still talking. There was no end to his supply of brilliant, dramatic lines. "You with the gun! I'm not fooling! Quick or I'll shoot!" And the click of the drawn-back hammer to punctuate the command.

Martell sighed and dropped his pistol, muzzle-first, so that if it discharged—which possibility didn't seem to have occurred to the boy, I suppose because they're always dropping guns harmlessly on TV—the bullet would go into the floor. Nothing happened. The weapon just bounced on the rug and lay still.

I had that terrible nightmare feeling you get when you see a very badly performed play or movie. Even when it's nothing to you if the performers make jackasses of themselves, it still hurts. I started to speak, to advise the boy but checked myself. All he had to do was pull a trigger, but that's something a kid's got to learn for himself, somehow.

They all think there's a kind of magic property in firearms, some hypnotic emanation that causes people to do your bidding. There isn't. The one thing a gun can do is shoot, and it isn't supposed to do even that without being told. But you can't explain it to them. They simply don't understand.

Joey was already moving now, very cautiously, increasing the distance between himself and Martell. I was going to have to decide very quickly whether or not to risk taking a hand.

"You there! I told you to stay put. . . !"

More words. Martell was moving. They were already far enough apart so that young Logan was having trouble keeping them both covered. The waving gun-barrel decided me. I wanted no part of this suicidal, sentimental foolishness. He wasn't really a bad kid, however, and I couldn't help pleading with him silently, for his own good: *You're going to have to shoot, you stupid little bastard. Why the hell don't you shoot now, while it will still do some good. . . ?*

But he couldn't do it, of course. It probably didn't even occur to him, really. He'd learned better, watching the 21-inch screen. You don't just up and kill a man standing there with his hands empty simply because he's moving his feet a little, for God's sake! Why, that's murder. . . . It was murder, all right. They whipsawed him expertly. I didn't see it all. When Joey set it off by lunging aside and going for his armpit gun, I threw a fast body-block into Beth and brought her down on the floor.

Then the boy was firing his silly carbine at Joey, in motion—now that he no longer had a stationary target, he was firing it!—and Martell was bringing my little .38 out of his pocket and shooting twice, and Joey, unscathed, was putting a third bullet into the boy, just out of meanness, as he hit the floor.

Beth scrambled out from under me and ran forward. Martell knocked her aside, thinking she was going for the fallen rifle, and maybe she was, but I doubt it. She wasn't weapons-oriented, if you know what I mean. He picked up the gun. She got up again and ran past him and went to her knees beside Peter Logan.

"He's still alive!" she gasped after a moment. "He's still breathing. . . . Please, can't you do something?"

"Fenn," Joey said pleadingly, "Fenn, can't you hear? The damn phone's ringing again!"

Chapter Twenty-one

JOEY SHOVED Beth forward, after dragging her out of the living room. She started to protest again, thought better of it, and picked up the phone.

"Yes," she said. "Yes, this is Mrs. Logan. . . ." A surprised look came to her face. "Who? Mr. Fredericks. . . ."

Martell reached out and took the instrument from her. "This is Fenn, Mr. Fredericks," he said and listened briefly. His gun, well out of reach from where I stood, never wavered. "We had some things to take care of before we could answer," he said. "Yes, Mr. Fredericks. Yes, everything is under control. . . . Sure, Mr. Fredericks, I'm listening."

He listened. Once, he laughed. Then he listened some more.

"I've got it," he said at last. "Four or five hours, you figure. Sure, Mr. Fredericks, we'll be ready for him. . . . No, you don't have to draw a diagram, he won't give you any more trouble. . . . What? Yes, we'll get that information for you, too. Sure, Mr. Fredericks. You can count on us. Yes, Mr. Fredericks, I understand. Yes, Mr. Fredericks. There won't be an ounce missing, I promise you. . . . Yes, we'll let you know as soon as. . . . Yes, Mr. Fredericks."

He hung up the phone and spat deliberately on the rug. His face was ugly. He swore fervently in a language I didn't understand. Then he remembered that he was supposed to be a guy named Fenn.

"Sonovabitch!" he said, with a quick glance at Joey. "I should have told him to take his lousy H and ram it up his . . . Where the hell do you think you're going, Duchess?"

She looked at him over her shoulder. "Somebody's got to—"

"Nobody's got to nothing," Martell said. The lapse into foreign obscenity seemed to have shaken him; now he was playing Fenn to the hilt. I was interested to see this. It meant that he wasn't too sure of how Joey would react to his real identity. He gave me a shove. "You get out to the car, quick, both of you, and watch yourselves. . . . You, Shorty, particularly! You aren't fooling me with that dumb and innocent look!"

I liked that. Whether as Fenn or Martell, he was having to remind himself, now, that he knew all about me, and that I was a potentially dangerous person. He'd taken me too easily, and Paul had probably been easy, too, and when I'd had a chance to act, just now, I'd taken shelter on the floor instead. It had been a long time since he'd had to deal with anything but policemen and hoodlums. It had been a long time since he'd had to deal with any of us, and then he'd done all right, in Berlin. His brain was warning him not to underestimate the enemy, but his ego was telling him these American agents weren't so much.

Beth said, horrified, "But you can't just leave the boy—"

Martell grinned at her. "No, I guess you're right. Joey, take your gun and go in there and finish him off. . . . That's what you meant, wasn't it, Duchess?"

She stared at the two of them, pale and wide-eyed; then she gave a little gasp and ran towards the front door. Martell laughed.

"After her, Joey. Keep an eye on her. I'll watch this one."

"But you said—" Joey had his gun out.

"Ah, the hell with the kid. He's not going anywhere. Let's get out of here." Martell gestured with the foreign automatic. "All right, Shorty. Slow and easy." He grinned at me as I moved past. "Just because The Man wants some information out of you doesn't mean you're bullet-proof. There's a lot of places I can shoot you where you'll live long enough to talk."

That answered one question: why I was still alive. It looked as if the day ahead might be long and eventful, not to say painful. Joey had disappeared outside. I walked slowly towards the door, and spoke without turning my head.

"Having fun, Vladimir?"

I heard him chuckle. "I make a very fine American gangster, do I not, Eric?"

"That foreign gun's a little out of character."

"Not at all. They are very popular among the people who are hep, as the saying goes. You must be new. I do not recall seeing your dossier, and I have a good memory."

I could have told him he just hadn't checked recently enough, or far enough back—they might still have something on me from the war, although we were supposed to be allies at the time—but it wasn't the place to boast of my vast and varied experience.

"I've seen yours," I said.

"That's very good," he said. "Then you know I do not fool when I tell you to be careful, very careful. No false moves. And no conversation with my Neanderthal assistant. If you should be thinking of trying to play on his patriotic sentiments by revealing me as a subversive person—"

"Has he got any sentiments, patriotic or otherwise? I saw no signs of them."

"You do him an injustice. I'm sure Joey is full of nice American sentiments about country and motherhood. If you try to talk with him, I will have to shoot you, even if it means that the objectionable Mr. Fredericks never finds his enchanting daughter. Where is she, by the way?"

"She's safe, for the time being."

He laughed. "So. Well, we have lots of time, Eric. It will give us something to do while we wait, finding out."

In passing, I glanced into the living room where young Logan lay near the fireplace. Well, I'd left better men in worse places. He seemed to be still breathing. You never know. One man will die from an infected hangnail, and the next will survive a machine-gun burst you'd think would kill a rhino.

Outside, Joey and Beth were waiting by a big Chrysler sedan that looked familiar. It was the same car in which I'd been brought to Fredericks the day before.

"She'll drive us," Martell said, jerking his head towards Beth. "You know the Buckman cabin, Duchess?" He was Fenn again. "Well, take us there. . . . Joey, you watch her close. I'll ride in back with Shorty."

We drove off in pale daylight. Twenty-four hours ago, I recalled, I'd been standing on a hill in the desert with a girl and a pair of binoculars, watching a dog catch a rabbit. Now the dog was dead, the girl hated me, and I was watching the sun come up in another place, waiting for some men to catch a man. The cast was different, but the script didn't seem to vary much. I heard Martell laugh softly to himself.

"That Duke must be quite a character," he said in Fenn's best voice. "You've got to hand it to him, cool as a breeze. The Man was telling me; he just got word from a spotter down on the border who saw him go through earlier. They stopped him at customs in that damned imported hot-rod and asked him if he had anything to declare. 'Why, certainly,' said the Duke, 'two quarts of tequila and a gallon of rum.' 'I'm sorry, sir,' said the customs guy, 'you're only entitled to bring in one gallon of alcoholic beverage; we'll have to ask you to take back the excess or pour it out.' 'I say, old chap, that does seem a pity, but the law is the law,' says the Duke, and he gets out and opens up the trunk and pours out the tequila casually—standing there with the trunk wide open and God knows how much horse in the spare tire! The spotter almost flipped, but the Duke never turned a hair. He closed the trunk, got back into that bomb of his, gave the guy a jaunty salute, and drove off smiling."

Joey said, "The spare tire? That's a hell of a corny place to hide it."

"Maybe, but he made it, didn't he? The Man says he should be here in four-five hours, the way he's pushing. . . . Keep your eyes on the road, Duchess."

Beth asked breathlessly, "What are you going to do to him?"

"Just drive, Gorgeous," Martell said. "You know what they say; ask a silly question, get a silly answer. That was a hell of a silly question, now, wasn't it?"

The old Buckman cabin was off the road a little ways, and the low Chrysler had a hard time making it over the ruts. Pretty soon they'll start building cars that you can't even get over the hump where your driveway meets the street. Beth stalled twice, braking hard for rocks and bumps.

Martell said, "Just goose it, Duchess. It's not your car, what the hell do you care what happens to The Man's muffler?"

We crashed and thrashed up to the place and went out and went inside. It wasn't much of a house, even for back in the mountains. Whoever the Buckmans had been, they'd moved out long ago. There was a cot, a table, and some wooden chairs in various stages of decay, in the largest room, the one we entered. There was a bedroom of sorts with a built-in double bunk visible through one door, and a kitchen with an old, wood-burning range visible through the other. There's nothing deader-looking than one of those old iron stoves rusting away from disuse.

"Over here, Duchess," Martell said, dusting off a chair with a flourish and taking her arm to seat her. His hand stayed a little longer and covered a little more territory than absolutely necessary. "Sit here and stay put."

Beth sat down, trying to ignore his touch. She had the prissy, head-high, eyes-forward look a certain kind of nice girl gets when she hears a wolf-whistle on the street. I hoped she didn't mean it. I hoped to God she didn't mean it. I was going to need her badly, soon.

Martell turned to me. "You," he said, "way over here. Now let's hear you talk. Where's Miss Fredericks? Where are you keeping her?" He looked down at me and sighed, and drew a pair of pigskin gloves from his pocket and started pulling them on. "Keep them covered, Joey," he said without turning his head. "This one wants it the hard way. . . ."

Chapter Twenty-two

IT WAS A long, rough morning, but I've known rougher. Martell's heart wasn't in it. He didn't really give a damn where I was hiding Moira Fredericks, and he wasn't in any hurry to find out—not yet, at least. He was just enjoying himself and incidentally, I noticed with hope, trying to impress Beth with what a big, tough, mean, irresistible man he was. I hadn't forgotten his record with the three black marks for falling down on the job on account of women.

I tried to signal her. It shouldn't have been necessary. A good female agent would have got to work on him as a matter of course. Even the Fredericks girl would have seen where her duty lay and done it without prompting, I was sure. But Beth continued to ignore Martell, deliberately and kind of desperately. I couldn't even catch her attention at first. She was doing her best not to watch the proceedings at all, which seemed fairly stupid. How did she expect us to get out of this if we didn't cooperate, and how were we going to cooperate if she wouldn't look my way for possible messages?

Finally I managed to establish communications and get the idea across. I saw her eyes widen incredulously. She glanced at Martell, and back at me, to be sure I really meant to ask this of her. Then, after a long pause, I saw her pull back her shoulders bravely, and, after another pause, raise her hands to her hair, which had become more than slightly disheveled during the course of the night and morning.

The next time he looked her way, she answered with a brief slanting glance, quickly withdrawn. There's nothing that beats, for pure coquettishness, that sidelong glance they give you while busy with their hair. I drew a sigh of relief. It looked as if I might make a soldier of

144

her yet. I even took courage from the fact that Martell was returning to the fray with renewed energy. Apparently, like many other men, he believed wholeheartedly in the theory that nothing made him bigger, in the eyes of a woman, than beating up another man in front of her.

Some time after eight o'clock I got a short respite when he sent Joey outside to keep watch.

"Logan will probably be coming from below," Martell said. "This road joins the main highway out on the desert somewhere. It would be his shortest route. But don't count on it. He might get tricky and swing up into the mountains and come down the way we came. Or he could park out of sight and sneak up on foot. So keep a sharp lookout." He watched Joey go out the door. Then he took out his gun and came back to me and kicked me in the shin. "Where were we? Oh, yes, you were going to tell me where you're keeping Miss Fredericks. . . ."

But the worst was over, for the time being. With Joey out of the room, he had to be careful about coming within reach; and he wasn't getting any real charge out of it now, anyway. His mind was busy elsewhere. He was listening.

When we heard the Jag coming at last, it sounded like a cross between a tractor-trailer rig pulling a steep grade and a buzz-saw slicing through soft pine. As it came closer, I could hear that the big six-cylinder mill was running rough. He needed new plugs all around after that long, hard drive, and a couple of valves needed attention badly. Joey appeared in the doorway.

"He's coming up the canyon!"

"All right," Martell said. "Now leave that door open and come over here and put your gun on this joker. The hell with what he knows. Don't monkey with him. If he moves, just shoot a nice big hole in him."

Joey pulled out his gun, a large revolver with an orifice in the barrel that was either .44 or .45 but looked considerably larger from where I was sitting. He showed it to me, so that if he had to use it I'd know what I'd been killed with, and walked around behind my chair where I couldn't see him without craning my neck, which didn't seem advisable. Besides, I wasn't going to strain any muscles I didn't have to. They were all pretty sore by this time.

Martell went over and pulled Beth to her feet. He was very business-like now, with action impending.

"All right, Duchess. Here's where you come in."

We could hear the Jaguar turning in from the canyon road, hitting bottom here and there on the primitive track leading to the cabin, as the Chrysler had done. Martell gave a sudden twist to Beth's wrist, levering it around and up between her shoulder blades.

"Joey," he said.

"Yeah."

"Watch him. I don't even want to have to think about him."

"I've got this monkey," Joey said. "You just handle the Duke. Be careful, he's supposed to know his way around."

Beth moaned slightly with the pain of her arm. "What are you going to—"

Martell said, "Play another record, Duchess. Or just shut up." He listened. The Jag had come to a stop outside. He shoved Beth roughly into the open doorway. "Duke," he called. "Duke Logan."

There was a little pause. I heard Joey cock his revolver, behind me. Then Logan's voice reached us, a little attenuated by distance. "I read you, old chap," the Duke said. "Loud and clear."

"You see what I've got here?"

"I see."

"Take out your gun and drop it on the ground. One careless move and I blow her spine in two."

There was another pause. Logan didn't say anything. There was nothing to say, although his kid would undoubtedly have made it the subject of six pages of corny dialogue. But the Duke had been raised in a harder school. The cards were dealt, the stakes were clear. He could either play out his hand, win or lose, or he could throw it in and hope for a better deal later—if he was an optimist.

The silence lasted for what seemed like a long time. Then we heard a little clinking sound as something metallic hit the dirt outside. It wasn't the choice I'd have made, but then, I've never liked postponing things, nor has chivalry ever been my ruling passion. The Duke, unlike me, was a gentleman.

Martell moved instantly. He knocked Beth aside, brought up his gun, and fired once. We heard, on the heels of the report, the slapping sound of the bullet striking flesh, the little involuntary gasp of the Duke as he was hit, and the sound of his body falling. Well, he must have known that would be the next thing. For a lady—his lady—he must have considered it worth while.

Martell drew a long breath, watching. "If you move one inch more, Duchess," he said without turning his head in the slightest, "you're going to need a set of false teeth, which would be a pity. . . . Joey."

"Yes."

"How's your patient?"

"Doing well, Fenn."

"Keep him covered, but come here."

There was a shuffling sound as Joey circled around me and backed towards the door.

"Duchess." Beth, crouched along the wall, her face shocked and white, didn't answer. Martell said sharply, "You're asking for it, Duchess! Right smack in the teeth. When I talk, you answer!"

"What . . . what do you want?"

"Get over there with your boyfriend. Not too close, not too far away. When I turn, I want to see two feet between you, no more no less. If there's a discrepancy, Gorgeous, I'll correct it with a bullet. You can have lots of fun guessing which one of you I'll shoot."

He still hadn't turned his head. He was keeping watch through the open door, pistol ready. He waited, as Beth moved across the room to me.

"Joey."

"Yes, Fenn."

"Are they over there? Together?"

"Yes."

"Okay. Now listen carefully. He's shamming uncon-scious right now, but all he's got is a bad leg. The gun's about a yard this side of him. I'd say it was out of his reach, but don't count on it. Anyway, he could be pack-ing another. Now you come here, tell me when you've got him covered, and I'll swing around to watch those two. . . . Okay?"

"Okay, Fenn, but—"

"But what?"

"Why just the leg? Why monkey with a guy like that, he's supposed to be a real—"

"Never mind the questions. Sing out when you've got him."

"I'm turning. . . . I've got him."

Martell pivoted sharply, bringing his gun to bear on us. He sidestepped, so that he was no longer in line with the door.

"Joey. Is he still playing dead?"

"He hasn't moved."

"All right. Now go out there and tell him this. Tell him I've got a bead on the dame again, and if I hear one single wrong sound behind me, I'll pull the trigger. . . . Then kick the gun away, frisk him, and drag him in here. Put him on the cot. Okay. Get going."

Joey vanished. We could hear his voice outside. After a little, he came into sight again, backwards, dragging Logan by the shoulders. He dragged him across the room and heaved him up on the cot. One of the Duke's legs hung at an odd angle, and his khaki pants-leg was stained with blood above the knee. Joey picked up the dangling leg and arranged it beside the other, with the fussy delicacy of an undertaker preparing a corpse.

Martell said, "Okay, Joey. Now go look in the trunk of his car. Bring in whatever you find there, like a spare tire full of something besides air."

We waited. Logan's heavy breathing was the loudest sound in the room. He hadn't opened his eyes, but I didn't think, any more than Martell, that he was unconscious, although being dragged around with a broken thigh-bone couldn't have been any fun. At that, he was lucky. Apparently none of the large blood vessels had been damaged, or there would have been a lot more blood and he wouldn't have been breathing much by this time. They go fast when the femoral artery is cut.

There was a sudden, scrambling sound outside, and Joey came running in. "Fenn! Fenn, it isn't there!"

"What isn't there?"

"The damn trunk's empty, except for a gallon of lousy Mex rum. There's no sign of the lousy spare tire!"

Chapter Twenty-three

LOGAN'S labored breathing didn't change rhythm. He was out cold with shock, to look at him: he hadn't heard a thing. Martell stared at Joey, and turned towards the cot. He walked closer and stood looking down at the wounded man. Slowly, his thick lips formed a grin.

"They told me you were tricky," he murmured. "Cute, real cute." He glanced at Joey again. "Now you see why we had to keep him alive? He came driving up here a little too innocent-looking for a man of his experience. I figured he must have left himself something to bargain with. . . . Stand still, Duchess!"

Beth said breathlessly, "But I've got to. . . . He'll bleed to death if you don't let me help him!"

Martell studied her for a moment. Then he nodded thoughtfully. "Yeah," he said. "Yeah, sure."

He reached into his pocket and brought out my little knife. He glanced at Joey to make sure the other man had everything under control. Joey nodded. Martell put his gun away, and opened the Solingen knife, and used the sharp blade to slit the Duke's trouser leg, baring the bullet-hole, from which blood was still welling thickly. He stepped back and tried to close the knife, but as I've said, it locks open. He glanced down irritably, looking for a catch. I opened my mouth to tell him how to do it —you press on the back of the small blade to let the large one close—but before I could speak, he'd snapped the knife in two and thrown the pieces aside.

Well, I'd done the same for Tony, so I suppose I had it coming, but it was a funny thing: it did what all the face-slapping and shin-kicking and general roughing-up hadn't succeeded in doing. I mean, that was all part of the job, but I'd carried the little knife a long time. It was an old friend and wartime comrade. It made things personal between Martell and me. He knew it, all right, and he gave me a kind of challenging glance, asking what I intended to do about it. I started to speak angrily, stopped, and lowered my glance quickly, letting him know I was afraid to antagonize him, lest he come over and hit me again.

Martell laughed. "All right, Duchess," he said, and gestured towards Logan. "Fix him up so he'll last a little while."

Beth had caught the silent exchange between us; she was looking at me in a half-puzzled, half-scornful way. I wasn't measuring up to what she'd expected of me; I wasn't making the right, courageous speeches. She turned at Martell's words.

"Yes," she said quickly, "of course." She walked rapidly to the cot, and I heard her breath catch as she saw the ugly wound at close range.

Martell had stepped back to let her by. Now he put his hands on her shoulders from behind. "They don't look like much, flat on their backs, do they?" She tried to shrug his hands away. She was looking around helplessly for something to use to stop the bleeding. Martell chuckled. "Is this what you need, Duchess?"

His hands closed on the collar of her blouse, and jerked apart and down. There was a shrill, ripping sound, and a stifled cry from Beth as the cloth cut into her here and there before yielding to the strain. Some buttons rolled on the floor. Martell opened his hands and let the wrecked blouse fall, in two halves, to her waist.

"There you are, Duchess. Plenty of bandages, but if you need more, we can probably find you some."

He was looking her over with a lot of pleasure, although I didn't see anything to merit all that attention. She didn't look very exciting to me as she freed herself from the torn silk: just a woman wearing a handsome chino skirt and, above the waist, a business-like brassiere more or less concealed by a nice, white, obviously quite expensive slip with some lace on it—attractive, but hardly world-shaking.

Martell licked his lips, however. Even Joey was interested, in his stolid way. Martell said, "Well, go on, Duchess."

She didn't look at him. She was examining a fistful of white silk, obviously closing her mind to the fact that it had very recently been a garment and forcing herself to think of it only as suitable raw material. . . . She tore it into strips, bandaged her husband's leg quite competently, and wiped her hands clean.

"There should be a splint to immobilize it," she said, straightening up.

"We won't bother with that," Martell said. "He's not going very far, if you know what I mean." He took her by the arm, clearly pleased that there was no longer a sleeve, even a thin one, to interfere with his enjoyment. In some ways, he was a man of very simple pleasures, Martell. "Now," he said, "you and I, Duchess, are going in the other room. We're going to have a lot of fun in there, until your husband chooses to wake up and tell us what he did with that tire—"

Beth's face had an incredulous and horrified look. I don't know why; she must have known it was coming. Maybe she'd closed her mind to that, too. She gave a sudden, frantic jerk and pulled away; then she was running for the door. With amateurs, it could have been a break, and I braced myself to come out of the chair, but Martell was no amateur. He had a weakness, serious for a man in his line of work, but he knew his business. He didn't waste a moment looking after Beth. His gun came out smoothly, and he took a backward step to a point from which he could cover both Logan and me.

He said, "Got her, Joey?"

Joey said, "Yeah, I've got her."

"Slap her down," Martell said without turning his head.

"Sure."

It had been a neat bit of team-play, Martell taking over responsibility for Logan and me while Joey, closer, instantly covered the door. Beth had run right into him. Now he held her off a bit with his left hand, and slapped her hard, twice.

Martell said, "That's enough. We don't want to spoil

her looks, eh, Joey? Don't worry. You'll get your turn. Now watch these two cute ones while I take her back in there and—"

Beth was sobbing helplessly, less with pain than with sheer terror. The sound annoyed me. I don't want to sound hard-boiled or anything, but I'd been taking a beating for several hours. Logan was on the cot with a badly injured leg. We all stood a good chance of dying if we didn't work together properly, and here she was making a big fuss about something of relatively little importance.

I mean, she was obviously going to be raped anyway. It had been inevitable since early that morning when she'd let them take the shotgun from her. I'd assumed she'd known it—hell, all she had to do was *look* at the guy—and was planning on it, figuring how best to make use of the fact that she was female, for the common good. I mean, it wasn't as if she were an innocent young virgin. She was a woman who'd had two husbands and three children. Why did she think I'd wigwagged her to play up to him, anyway?

I guess the fact is that I'd been counting on her as I'd have counted on a good female agent in the same spot—or any woman with courage and good sense, for that matter. I'd been depending on her to take Martell out of the play and be real nice to him when the opportunity presented itself, like now, long enough for me to put in some propaganda work on Joey, who was long on experience and know-how, but a little short on brains.

But it was fast becoming obvious that the thought hadn't crossed her mind, or that if it had, she'd dismissed it as something too horrible to be seriously considered. A provocative glance or two, maybe, even a smile, perhaps, but if anybody seriously expected her to go into that room with this vile man and entertain him. . . . Well! How disgusting could you get, anyway? I wasn't going to get any help from her, that was abundantly clear.

At the moment, I would gladly have traded her, and three more like her, for just one kid I could remember, named Tina, who'd have put up a fight, sure, who'd have sobbed and pleaded, perhaps, but who would have yielded at just the right moment, reluctantly at first and then enthusiastically, as if she couldn't help herself, making Martell feel big and strong and virile and irresistible, keeping him busy and happy until she could get her hands on his gun and blow his brains out. With Tina, I'd have had nothing to worry about except Joey. Martell would never have come out of that room alive. . . .

Well, Tina was dead. As a matter of fact, I'd had to kill her myself, under orders, the way you kill a savage female watchdog that starts biting the wrong people. It was Tina's death last year, and Beth's stumbling upon the unpleasant scene although she'd been warned to stay away, that had led to the break up of our marriage. At the moment, disappointed and disillusioned and a little scared, knowing it all depended on me now, I couldn't really see how I'd come to marry the fool woman in the first place.

Joey had us men covered. Martell had Beth by the arm again, and was pulling her across the room.

"Please!" she was crying, holding back desperately, "oh, please. . . !"

I mean, it was really kind of a silly performance, from a grown woman. I'd known teen-aged girls in France, nice, sheltered young girls, who'd done much better when the Nazis came, without a fraction of Beth's knowledge and experience. Her terror was too much for the Duke. Whatever he'd had in mind, playing dead—it was a gambit with good possibilities—he gave it up right then.

"That won't be necessary," he said, opening his eyes and pushing himself up on the cot. "The spare wheel you want is five miles back down the road, five-point-three by my odometer. Look for a ravine on the south side. You may have to climb down a ways. Wheels roll, don't you know?"

Chapter Twenty-four

JOEY MADE IT in about half an hour. It seemed longer, and I won't guarantee that it wasn't, since I didn't feel like attracting Martell's attention by moving my arm unnecessarily to check my wristwatch—but as a photographer I used to be able to call off intervals of time with fair accuracy, and I'd say half an hour.

At the end of it, even Martell was showing signs of strain. After all, a Jaguar uses a fairly large wheel, and a Jag spare tire can hold a lot of heroin which can be sold for a lot of money, a fact which might percolate even into Joey's dim brain. Of course, Martell had had no choice. If he'd gone after it himself, that would have left us free to work on Joey with threats and blandishments. . . .

The rest of us weren't very relaxed and cheerful, either. I kept my attention more or less on Logan. The guy was supposed to be good, and if he had any ideas, I didn't want to miss them, but all he did was lie on his back and stare at the ceiling. His face was shiny with sweat. I guess his leg was starting to give him hell.

On the other side of me, in a chair, Beth sat bare-armed and bare-shouldered, trying to assume the casual look of the girls in the corset and girdle ads who float around in their underwear as naturally as if nobody ever wore anything else. I'd paid some attention to her at the start, wondering if I'd misjudged her and if she could have been putting on a deliberate panic act for some reason, but all I saw in her eyes was a dull terror too real to be assumed. There weren't going to be any bright ideas from her.

There weren't going to be any bright ideas from anybody. The age of miracles was over. It was all up to Mrs.

Helm's little boy Matthew, who sometimes played cops and robbers under the code name Eric.

We heard the Chrysler turn in from the canyon road and come crashing up to the cabin. Joey hurried inside, holding the Jag's spare wire wheel in a loving embrace. He carried it forward tenderly and placed it on the table.

He'd already, apparently, pried the tire loose from the rim on one side. Now he pulled the rubber aside and produced a shiny, friction-top, tin can, which he set down in front of him. Then he reached in his pocket and came up with a screwdriver he'd probably got from the Jaguar's toolkit. All those British cars come equipped with enough tools to rebuild them from scratch.

Martell put one hand on the can and grasped Joey's wrist with the other. Joey looked up, surprised and hurt.

"I'll do it," Martell said.

"Okay, okay," Joey said.

Martell took the screwdriver and pried open the can. "Keep an eye on them, damn it!" he said sharply.

"Okay, okay!" Joey said, turning to face us.

Martell stuck a finger into the can. I noted that he seemed to poke deeper than necessary, as if he were feeling for something.

"How is it?" Joey asked, watching us.

Martell found what he was searching for. I saw his face go smooth with relief. He withdrew his finger, and tasted the white powder that clung to it, and spat.

"Not bad," he said. "They haven't cut it much." He slapped the lid back on the can and drove it home with his fist. "How many are there?"

"I didn't count. The whole damn tire's full of them."

"All right," Martell said. "Put it back. That Fredericks is a suspicious bastard; if he sees we've had it open, he'll be sure we've had a fix out of it, at least—as if I'd touch the lousy stuff!"

Joey hesitated. "Fenn."

"Yeah."

"That's a lot of horse. What's it bring, around a grand an ounce?"

"So?"

"I was just thinking—"

"Nobody ever got hurt just thinking," Martell said. "Not until they started doing something about it. Did you have in mind doing something about it, Joey?"

"Well, no, but—"

"Then stick it back in the tire like I told you and stop dreaming. Okay. Now I want you to keep a sharp eye on these characters while I tend to some unfinished business. . . . Duchess!"

Beth's head came up quickly. Martell walked over to stand above her. He looked her up and down, and licked his heavy lips.

"Do you walk or do I drag you?" he asked. "You're a big girl now, Mrs. Logan. You don't want these men of yours to see you dragged across the floor like a baby, kicking and screaming. . . . That's better."

She got up very slowly. She looked at Logan, still staring at the ceiling with the sweat of agony running off his face, and she looked at me. She looked at me longer, I guess, because I had two good legs and might get a little farther before the bullet from Joey's big revolver cut me down. Then she drew a long, shuddering breath and started across the room, and stopped.

"Larry!" she whispered. "Matt!"

Nobody said anything. She started walking again. Suddenly Logan moved. I heard the click as Joey cocked his revolver, and Martell's gun was in his hand. Logan fell back to the cot with a groan, his face gray and wet.

"Helm!" he said. "For God's sake!"

I still couldn't see that it was worth getting killed for. Well, to prevent it, maybe, but nobody was going to prevent it, and I never could get excited about the idea of dying nobly for nothing.

I said, "You're the husband now. You want to be a dead hero, go ahead."

He said, "I can't. . . . We're all going to be dead, old man, don't you know that?"

"I've known it for years," I said. "I'll still wait for the time."

Joey chuckled. He sat down at the table, resting the gun on the big wire wheel lying there.

"Go on, Fenn," he said. "Have your fun. They ain't giving me no trouble. None that I can't handle."

Martell said, in his best Fenn voice, "Nobody's dying for you today, Duchess. Too bad."

Beth licked her lips, pulled her shoulders back, and walked straight into the bedroom. He followed her and closed the door. It didn't take long. There wasn't time enough for me to even begin talking to Joey, without looking as if I was rushing things.

He was wide open for it. I could have worked on his greed, which he'd just betrayed, and dressed it up pretty with an appeal to his patriotism. I could have worried him badly just by letting him know I was a government man. Ever since Dillinger they've had a kind of superstitious fear of the G-men, and I wouldn't have to mention that I didn't happen to be working for J. Edgar Hoover. . . . But she gave me no time at all.

Suddenly the door opened and she came out, looking, except for the expression of her eyes, exactly as she'd looked going in. She hadn't even got her hair badly mussed, not enough that she hadn't been able to pat it back into place. Except for the missing blouse, and the frozen look in her eyes, she looked as if she'd just been for a stroll around the house.

Martell was behind her, and he looked angry and unsatisfied. I knew exactly what she'd done. She'd undressed for him fast and let him have her, to get it over with, since she had no choice, but she'd given him no more than he could have got from a properly constructed store-window dummy. In the years to come, if she lived that long, she'd take pride in the fact, no doubt. He'd had her body but he hadn't touched her soul. Not that she was likely to live that long. None of us were, now.

He grabbed her and stopped her. I saw his glance touch the wheel on the table before it came to rest on Joey.

"Okay, Joey," he said. "Your turn." He rubbed his

head ruefully. "Watch that damn upper berth or you're like to knock your brains out."

Beth's stony expression didn't change. She just stood there. Joey looked at her for a moment. It was hard to say what went through his mind, such as it was. Maybe, like me, he'd seen the direction of Martell's first glance, and got a vague hunch it might be best for him not to leave again. And I suppose he could tell that Lover-Boy Fenn hadn't gone over real big in there. Maybe he just didn't figure it was going to be worth the trouble for him to try. But I don't discount the possibility that he had some kind of decency. This was a woman from a different world, and he'd just stick to his own kind, thanks.

"I'll pass it, Fenn," he said.

Martell looked surprised and annoyed. He started to speak sharply, stopped, and shrugged his shoulders. "Suit yourself. I can tell you you're not missing much." He gave Beth a shove. "Go on back over there and sit down."

Joey glanced at his watch. "We'd better get on a phone and report to Mr. Fredericks that we've got it, before he starts getting impatient."

Martell said, "Yeah, sure, as soon as we finish what he sent us to do." He walked up to me and kicked me hard in the shin. He seemed to have a knack for hitting the same place every time. I let him know it hurt. "All right," he said. "I'm through horsing around, Buster. Where's Miss Fredericks?"

I said, "I'm not going to tell—"

He moved in fast and hard, slugging, chopping with the edge of his hand, slapping, kicking. I covered up as best I could and rolled with the worst ones, riding it out: this didn't mean anything, either. This was just Martell taking it out on me because a pretty woman hadn't responded properly to his advances. Or maybe he was just stalling while he figured things out.

Pretty soon we'd settle down to the lighted-cigarette routine, or he'd send Joey for a pair of pliers. And when Joey came back, he might possibly walk into a bullet—from my gun, to make it look good later, or Logan's, but that was lying outside somewhere. In any case, there was something in that tire beside heroin that Martell wanted, and he obviously wanted to get it without having Joey tell all about it later. And since Joey had been so foolish as to refuse to retire gracefully from the room, something might very well happen to him, as it was going to happen to all of us. Meanwhile, Martell was putting on a show, as Fenn, while he made up his mind.

I drew back from a punch in the eye, and the ancient chair groaned and collapsed, sending me over backwards. It was a chance, but I threw a glance towards the table as I went over, and Joey had the .45 trained on me rock-steady. There was nothing to do but cover up some more, as Martell moved in for some fancy kicking.

I waited, curled up on the floor, but the kick didn't come. Instead, there was a high, crazy peal of laughter. I looked up. Beth had got up from her chair. Martell, sensing attack, had jumped back instinctively, but she had no time to spare for him. She was staring down at me, but her hands were clapped over her mouth, as if the sudden, wild laughter had startled even her. She took them down and giggled.

"Look at him!" she breathed. "Look at him, the big dangerous man, the man I divorced because . . . because I was afraid of him, God help me!"

It didn't seem like anything that required a reply. I merely picked myself up with as much dignity as I could muster. Then the idea came to me and I made an ineffectual gesture of protest.

"Now, Beth——"

"Now, Beth!" she mimicked, taking a step forward. "Now, Beth!"

"Now, Beth," I said mildly, "you're just upset because——"

"Upset!" she gasped. Her eyes were suddenly wide and a little mad. "Because! I suppose it's nothing to be upset about? And what did you do to prevent it? You just sat there and said you didn't want to be a dead hero."

I was watching her closely, looking for some hint,

some sign, some signal that she was acting, but there was not. She was perfectly serious, in an overwrought way. She meant every word, so I'd have to play it on that basis.

I noted that Martell had pulled back near the table, behind me. My one glance told me that he was grinning. She'd made him feel like a lower form of life. Now it was somebody else's turn, and he liked it. He thought it was very funny; funny enough to watch for a while, just for laughs. Joey thought it was funny, too, but he was worried about how much time we were wasting. Mr. Fredericks would be getting impatient—and it wasn't wise to keep The Man waiting.

I said, "Beth, really! What did you expect me to do—"

"Do," she breathed, taking another step forward. "Do? I expected you to do something, anything! Larry would have done it, if he could!"

I said angrily, drawing back a step, "Larry's already had a leg shot from under him because of you! I suppose he would have been fool enough to get himself killed because of you!"

"Yes," she hissed, "yes, you would think that was foolish, wouldn't you, darling?"

I showed my teeth in something that was supposed to be a ratty grin. I said viciously, "What the hell are you squawking about, darling? There's Larry with a smashed leg. Here am I after a four-hour beating, and just what the hell, may I ask, is wrong with you? Nothing that, at the worst, can't be fixed by a small routine operation and a few shots of penicillin! Oh, and a visit to a good psychiatrist, if you're going to take it that big! I mean, just what the hell gives you the right to—"

It worked. I wasn't proud of it, I wouldn't want to have to do it again, but it worked. This was Beth, the girl you couldn't quarrel with, but I guess everybody's got a breaking point somewhere. She came for me then, clawing and scratching, spitting and snarling and kicking, calling me names I hadn't suspected her of knowing.

I covered up and backed away, hearing Martell laughing heartily behind me. I heard his laughter stop, but he'd made his mistake. He'd forgotten I was supposed to be dangerous. I'd worked hard for that forgetting, I'd paid high for it, but it was worth the price. When he realized his error, he was too late, I was too close. I was right there.

I dumped the table on top of Joey. The big Jaguar wheel helped. Sliding off, it took him right in the chest. I turned, and my timing was perfect. The gun was just coming out from under Martell's coat. I gave it to him right in the solar plexus; the dagger-thrust with the stiffened fingers that's worse than the blow of a fist. He doubled up, paralyzed, and I had the gun.

I shot him with it once and threw myself down, and Joey's first shot went over me. It was all he was entitled to. It was close range and I could aim for the head. The first bullet just punched a neat round hole, but the second kind of blew things apart a little. Scratch Joey, who'd had one good impulse in his life, if it was that. Well, many of them don't even have one.

I got up. Martell seemed to be still breathing, and I kind of kept an eye on him, but I was more worried about Joey's single wild shot, at the moment. Beth was sitting on the floor nearby. I went over and lifted her. She was making small, mindless, whimpering noises.

"Are you all right?" I asked. "Are you hit?"

The funny thing was, my worry was quite genuine. A minute or two ago, I wouldn't have given a nickel for her, with or without shirt, but now that it was over, more or less, I didn't want her to have been hurt. She didn't answer. She just kept on sobbing in a disconnected way.

Logan's voice spoke calmly: "The stray bullet struck the wall over here. Elizabeth is merely a bit hysterical, don't you know?"

I knew, all right. I'd be wearing the scratches to prove it for days to come. I helped her across the room. She sat down on the cot beside Logan and buried her face in her hands.

"And you?" I asked him.

"Feeling quite fit," he said. He glanced at his wife.

"You were a bit hard on her, old boy. It's not something women take in their stride, you know."

"It would be difficult to do," I said. "But no doubt it's been tried."

He looked a little baffled; then he said, "Ah, yes. Quite." Then he said, calmly, "You'd better attend to our friend over there. I believe he is reaching for another weapon. At least he is still alive."

"I can't see any necessity for that," I said, and I went over and shot Martell through the back of the head. I mean, it was the only thing to do. We weren't completely out of the woods yet, as I saw it; there was work left to be done. With his wound, Logan could pass out any time, and I couldn't trust Beth to look after a tame rabbit.

I heard her gasp, behind me. Apparently she'd come out of it enough to witness my brutal act. Even Logan seemed disturbed.

"I say, old boy—"

I turned Martell over with my foot. He'd been curled up on the floor like a baby, but he straightened out as he rolled over limply, and his hand swung outward, holding the little .38 revolver he'd taken from me earlier in the day. You had to hand it to the guy. He'd had the old team spirit. They'd slapped his face and sent him to Siberia—or America—but he'd still been right in there trying, to the end.

I reached down and took the revolver from his fingers. stuck his gun into my pocket, and got out spare shells to reload the two fired chambers of my own—the ones he'd used on young Logan. That was something I was going to have to break to the Duke, or somebody was, but this didn't seem like just the time. I looked down at the dead face with the thick sexy lips without any particular satisfaction.

It had been a personal matter, and it was settled. Paul was avenged, and so was a guy named Francis I'd never met. Come to that, you couldn't really say that Paul had been a very close friend of mine. However, Mac could relax and Smitty could transfer the card to the closed file. But I was still going to miss that little knife.

I sighed, and went to the tire on the floor, got out one of the shiny cans, found the screw-driver, and pried off the lid. I poked around in the white stuff, and drew out, cautiously, a small dull metal cylinder. It was quite heavy, and I could scratch the metal with my thumb-nail, which seemed to make it lead. Two small wires, neatly coiled, were attached to one end of the cylinder.

Beth had got up to look. "What is it?" she asked.

"I don't know," I said, "but I don't think it would be a good idea to touch the ends of those wires together, at least not with a battery in the circuit."

"But I don't understand—"

"That makes two of us," I said.

Logan's voice was lazy: "I say, old boy—"

I was getting very tired of that accent, phony or genuine. "What is it, old boy?"

"There seems to be a car coming down the canyon. Can't be sure it's headed here, of course, but nevertheless—"

"Oh, Lord!" I said reverently.

We weren't out of the woods, but at least I was beginning to see daylight through the trees ahead. I tucked the little lead cylinder back into its heroin nest, and put the lid back on the can. This gave me something to do while I figured my tactics. You don't ever want to let anyone know you haven't got the answers right at your fingertips.

Then I went over and dropped Martell's automatic on Logan's cot and went out of the cabin without giving any stupid instructions. If he was as good as he was supposed to be—which we'd seen no signs of yet—he'd think of something intelligent to do. If he couldn't think of it himself, he probably wouldn't do it right if I told him.

They came in beautifully, like ducks to the decoys. I was up above them on the hillside, behind a bush, as they bounced into range in their long, air-conditioned Cadillac. There was Fredericks and a driver, the man

I'd once seen guarding the door of Fredericks' office at the hotel. They drove right up below me and got out and looked around.

"Both cars are here," I heard Fredericks say. "I wonder what the hell—"

From inside the cabin came the shrill, outraged scream of a woman. Logan had thought of something, and Beth had done it. I'd have to pin medals on both of them, later.

The driver laughed. "No wonder they were too busy to hear us coming."

Fredericks said angrily, "Damn it, they can do their womanizing on their own time! I'll teach them to keep me waiting."

I had the driver covered, figuring him to be more dangerous. Fredericks wouldn't have been doing his own shooting for years. It should have been an easy touch, but I had to go and remember Mac's words: *at least a semblance of legality, to keep our brother agencies happy.* I stood up behind my bush.

"Put your hands up!" I said. "You're both under arrest!"

It was a stupid damn business. There must be some good way of doing it—cops do it all the time, I hear—but obviously that wasn't it. They both dove in different directions, going for their guns.

I got the driver all right, leading him nicely, so that he lunged right into the path of the bullet. Then I swung for Fredericks, and something hit me a hard and paralyzing blow in the right side of the chest.

I tried for the gun with my left hand. There's a stunt known as the Border Shift whereby you transfer a weapon from one hand to the other—a kind of juggling trick. The only trouble is, it doesn't work too damn well when your right arm's out of commission, and when else do you need it? The last time it was actually tried in action, on the record, as far as I know, was when Luke Short, an old-time gambler and a tough one, clipped the hand of some wild-shooting drunk, who then tried the

Shift, too, but he didn't make it, either. Luke shot him dead.

I felt the revolver drop, and I threw myself on top of it, still trying to find it left-handed. I didn't have much time. I could feel the gun trained on me and I wondered where this one would hi: . . . .

There was a shot all right, and another, but no bullets came near me. I picked up the .38 and looked up. Fredericks was standing there with an odd, slack look on his face, doing nothing whatever. He dropped the gun he was holding. Then he started to fall.

I looked towards the cabin. Well, he had to be good for something, the reputation he had around that place. . . . It was the shoulder-holster man, the great white hunter, old Bwana Simba himself coming out of retirement, a beautiful sight. How he'd made it to the door on a shattered leg, even with Beth to help him, I didn't know. I didn't intend to ask. He'd just give me some of that stiff-upper-lip, British guff.

He was shooting very carefully, making target practice of it, body as relaxed as his wound allowed, arm extended but not locked. He put two more into The Man as he fell, with deliberate accuracy, making quite sure. He'd been in the business once, himself.

I got up. My chest didn't seem to hurt much. That would come later. I went over and checked the Duke's work, and my own. I made my way to where he still leaned in the doorway. Beth was beside him, steadying him. I looked at the two of them, and spoke to him.

"That was pretty fair country shooting, old chap," I said. "While we still have some privacy, you might let me know how much of this you want credit for, on the books."

He looked me straight in the eye. "None, if it can be arranged," he said.

I thought of various things, and said, "We could probably get you a small medal or some nice words from Uncle or something."

He glanced at Beth. "We would rather not figure in it at all, if it's possible," he said, and she nodded. He smiled faintly. "I would certainly prefer not to be re-membered as the man who smuggled a certain number of pounds of heroin, not to mention that other material, across the Mexican border. If it's all the same to you, old man."

It wasn't the same to me, not quite, but the guy had saved my life—at least I thought so at the time. There were occasions during the next couple of weeks when I wasn't quite so sure. . . .

Chapter Twenty-five

THE YOUNG MAN from the AEC said, "Of course, Mr. Helm, you understand all this is highly confidential."

"Oh, sure," I said. "What was in those cans, anyway? Their new pocket model atomic bomb?"

"Well," he said reluctantly, "not quite. It was . . . a very ingenious sabotage device consisting of radioactive wastes enclosed in a shielded container with a small bursting charge. The explosive wasn't sufficient to do much damage, but it would distribute the radioactive material over a fairly wide area, with unfortunate results to anyone who happened to be standing nearby, particularly if he didn't realize the danger and undergo decontamination immediately. We've had a few cases . . ."

"I know," I said. "I read the papers."

"There have been others, less fatal, that didn't reach the papers," he said. "In many cases, with prompt action, the injury was relatively slight—the physical injury that is. But the injury to morale has been serious." He frowned. "You must understand, Mr. Helm, that people who work around nuclear reactions tend to be, well, let's say, a bit sensitive about anything pertaining to radioactivity. Just like people working around high explosives tend to jump unnecessarily at loud noises. When things start to burst that shouldn't, if you know what I mean, and when people find themselves receiving heavy contamination in places that are supposed to be relatively safe. . . . Well, it cuts down the efficiency, to say the least. One installation, just the other day, couldn't even get the trash removed until the workers were permitted to don full protective clothing. Things like that. It was a fiendishly clever device, psychologically speaking. If they'd got enough of them . . ."

168

I looked at the bright window, through which, since I was on the second floor of the hospital, I could see only the blue and cloudless Nevada sky.

"Shielded, you say," I said. "How much shielding do you get from that little bit of lead?"

He laughed. "You don't have to worry, Mr. Helm. You've been checked, very thoroughly. Although you handled one of the bombs, you apparently didn't get enough exposure to do any damage. It was only when the contents were actually splashed on someone that the situation was urgent and dangerous. However, if some gentleman down in Mexico slept with the entire supply under his bed, he might be feeling a little unwell by now. And I don't know as I'd care to shoot that heroin into my veins, even if I was addicted to the stuff. Of course, that was their difficulty. Any normally sensitive instrument would have detected the hot material through the relatively inadequate lead shield, which is why they brought it in by such roundabout channels."

I said, "Silly question, but why didn't they just make up the nasty little things right here in the country?"

"Where would they get the critical ingredient? We don't sell it over the counter, you know. It would have had to be imported, anyway; and the device is not one anybody could put together in a cellar from a gas pipe and a few sticks of dynamite." He rose. "Their experiment was a success; let's say the first shipment, with which we're still dealing, went over big. If they'd got hold of the second shipment and got it planted before we understood what we were up against, we'd have been in real trouble. As it is, of course, we can take precautions against further sabotage of this nature—although I think it's probably the first time we've had to worry about anybody bringing radioactive materials *onto* an atomic installation. Coals to Newcastle, eh? Well, good-bye, Mr. Helm. Your chief wanted me to let you know the background, as soon as you were well enough. I hope I haven't tired you too much."

I watched the door close behind him. It was interesting information, to be sure, but I didn't really know what good it was to me. I went to sleep. In the morning, Beth came to see me.

She entered the room a little uncertainly, as if not quite sure she'd be welcome. She was wearing one of those artificially faded denim skirt-and-shirt outfits and her big white Stetson hat. I was glad when she took the hat off and didn't look quite so much like a rodeo girl.

"The nurse said it was all right for me to look in, if I didn't stay too long," she said. "How are you feeling, Matt?"

"Fine," I said. "Well, more or less. How about you?"

She looked surprised that I'd ask. "Why, I'm fine," she said, and then she realized what I was driving at, and flushed slightly. "I'm fine," she said again. "I . . . I'm all right. Really." She laughed quickly. "I suppose you know the Logan family has been in a bad auto accident."

"Is that the way they handled it?"

"You didn't know?"

"I just passed the word before they started digging lead out of me," I said. "I didn't know just how they'd work it out."

"We smashed up the Jaguar in Buckman Canyon," she said, "with the three of us crowded aboard. Anyway, that's the story. Fortunately there happened to be some law-enforcement officers around. We never did learn just what they were doing there, of course, but they were very kind and considerate and got Peter and Larry to the hospital right away. One of the officers even contributed his uniform blouse." She was silent for a moment; then she went on: "'Your boss seems to be a man of influence. The doctors haven't said a word about bullet wounds. The papers just reported the 'accident' in a few lines. I . . . we're very grateful, Matt. If there had been any publicity, it would never have been . . . well, *right,* again. You know what I mean. He's been trying to live it all down. He doesn't want to be a hero, any more than a villain. He just wants to be a . . . a peaceful, law-abiding citizen, an ordinary person. I thought he'd be sad because he'd had to sacrifice the Jaguar, but he says it's just as well, he's got no business driving a car like that.

He's going to be strictly the family-sedan type from now on."

"I know," I said. I'd been the pickup-truck type for years, with the same motives, but it hadn't taken. But I didn't say that. "Tell him I wish him luck," I said.

"And me?" she asked.

"You too," I said. "Naturally."

She smiled. "You were pretty disgusted with me there for a while, weren't you? I don't really blame you. I didn't behave very well, by your standards. Fortunately, Larry's more interested in a wife and companion than in a . . . a hunting partner, if that's the right word. And I'm a pretty good wife and companion, Matt, even if I'd make a terrible secret agent."

I grinned. "Terrible is right. Well, anyway, it's nice we both know for sure, isn't it? There was a moment when I first saw you, a few weeks back. . . ."

"Yes," she said, "if the boys hadn't interrupted . . ." She shivered slightly. "Thank God they did!"

I said, "You don't have to be so emphatic about it. You might hurt my feelings."

She laughed. She wasn't worried about my feelings. After watching me shoot Martell through the head, she probably wasn't too sure I really had any. She picked up her big hat. "Well, I'd better. . . ."

I said, "Just one thing, Beth."

She turned at the door. "What's that?" she asked.

"Those two men," I said, "the ones who tried to perform a kidnaping and got eaten by a dog, remember?" I wouldn't have brought it up, if she hadn't laughed like that.

She licked her lips. "How could I forget? Why . . . why did you mention it?"

"Because you sent them," I said. I waited, but she didn't speak. I said, "I've been thinking about the times and mileages involved, and there's no other answer. Larry was already well on his way to the Mexican border, he had to be, when those men came for Moira Fredericks; and Larry isn't the kind to run off and leave his wife to supervise a kidnaping alone. He wouldn't have let you

have any part in it, assuming that he'd pull a stunt like
that in the first place. It's my feeling that, unlike some
people we know, Larry's really too much of a gentleman to
use a young girl he knows and likes as a weapon against
her father."

She said, "You're calling him Larry now. You used to
insist on calling him Duke."

"He's earned the right to be called what he wants by
me," I said. "And you're changing the subject. My guess
is that your quarrel with Larry was much earlier in the
day than you let me think, maybe right after he'd sent
the kids up into the mountains that morning. You got
into an argument about how safe they'd be there, probably; and that's when he stalked to the phone and called
up Fredericks and drove off mad. Then you started feeling guilty about being the cause of his giving in like that.
He'd left a couple of tough boys to look after you, telling
them to take orders from you. And you had this bright
idea, only it didn't quite work out."

She licked her lips again. "I was only trying to . . . to
help. To make it unnecessary for him to go through
with . . . I thought, if we had the girl, we could make
some kind of deal when he got back. . . ." She drew a
long breath. "You're right, of course. It was a crazy,
terrible thing to do. I still wake up at night, seeing . . .
What are you going to do about it, Matt?"

"Does Larry know?"

"Of course he knows."

I said, "Don't worry about me. I just thought I'd set
the record straight, between us. May I ask a question?"

"Yes," she said. "Of course."

"Think hard now. Would you ever have dreamed of
sending some men to kidnap anybody for my sake?"

She hesitated. Then she said in a small voice, "I don't
think so, Matt."

"Then everything is fine the way it is, isn't it?"

She nodded. "Everything is fine."

"Well," I said, "give my love to the kids. I'll try to remember their birthdays from time to time."

"Larry says . . . he says his objections are withdrawn,

of course, and you're welcome at the ranch any time."

"Sure."

She hesitated, but we'd said just about everything necessary, and she turned and walked out of the room. I lay back and thought about the kids I wouldn't be seeing much of. Well, I'd never been very active in the papa department, anyway. Logan would probably work much harder at it. I guess I must have gone to sleep, because suddenly the kid was standing at the foot of the bed, looking at me.

She was wearing a black linen suit and black shoes and gloves and she looked smart but rather subdued, for her. Her red-gold hair was just as smooth and bright as it could be, not a tendril out of place. Maybe she'd stopped outside to fix it, and maybe she was just growing up. Maybe she really had it licked at last. Her sea-green eyes said she'd done some growing since I'd seen her last.

"Hello, Moira," I said.

"Hello, baby."

"I thought you were mad at me."

"That was a couple of weeks ago," she said. "I don't stay mad that long." After a moment, she said, "You certainly look helpless in that bed." Then she said: "My mother died the other day."

"I'm sorry."

"Cut it out," she said. "Why should you be sorry? She was just waiting, I guess. She was going to outlast him. When she heard about him, there wasn't anything else to keep her, and she just went, I guess." She made a gesture towards her somber clothes. "Mourning. Corny, huh?"

I said, "I thought it was for—"

"For him? I wouldn't change my socks for him." After a moment, she said, "Did you have to do it?" Then she glanced at the bulk of the bandages under my hospital gown. "I guess that's a silly question. But—" She drew a long breath. "You know what I mean."

"Yes."

"Well, it was pretty good for a little while," she said flatly. "Choice."

"Yes," I said. "Choice."

"I could bring you flowers or candy or something. Should I?"

"No."

"I kind of thought that's what you'd say."

I said, "They tell me young Logan is down the hall. He's still on the critical list. A little incentive might help."

She looked at me without expression. "You may be a pretty good whatever you are," she said. "But you're a hell of a lousy matchmaker. Why don't you mind your own damn business?"

"It was just a stray thought."

"No wonder it strayed. Nobody'd bother to round up one like that." She drew a long breath. "What room?"

"A hundred and thirty-four."

"I'll see how he's getting along. Just to please you." She studied me for a moment longer. "You know, the old man never did anything right in his life, did he? He couldn't even shoot straight! If he'd killed you, I could grieve for you. It would be a damn sight easier than . . . Good-bye, baby."

"Good-bye," I said, and watched her go out of the room quickly, noting that a little wisp of red-gold hair was coming down over her right ear. She hadn't grown up quite enough to lick it, after all. Well, she had lots of time.

I could have told her that I hadn't actually killed her old man, of course, although I'd been working at it hard. I might have kept her around for a while, that way. It would have been nice; but it wasn't my secret, and there was nothing I could give her of much value, compared to what she had to give to somebody, now that she was free. I was being noble, I guess. As usual, it made me feel lousy, and I was glad when the telephone rang; but when I heard the voice at the other end, I was less glad than I had been.

Mac's voice asked, "How are you, Eric?"

I said, "For an accurate diagnosis, check with the attending physician."

"I have. He says you'll live."

"Well, I'm glad he's finally made up his mind," I said.

"When you're well enough, I'd like a full report," Mac said. "There seem to be a few matters requiring detailed explanation. In the past fortnight I've had to think up stories to account for two juvenile delinquents with damaged right arms, six dead human bodies, one dead canine body, one irate young woman held prisoner against her will, three badly wounded men, and a lady without a shirt on."

I said, "Not to mention a few kilos of heroin, and some other stuff."

"Yes," he said. "There's that, isn't there? Our associated agencies, although professing to be shocked by the methods used, are quite pleased with the results obtained."

"And you, sir?"

"What do you think, Eric? The information I have indicates that one of my men allowed himself to be a) knocked on the head, b) captured in his sleep, and c) shot by a man he already had covered."

I said, "Your information seems to be quite complete, sir. What are you going to do, fire me in disgrace and send me off to Siberia, or its equivalent, to run a post office?"

He was silent briefly; then he said, "That was it, wasn't it, Eric? That was what Martell was doing all those years, looking after the mail. No wonder he resented it, after the position he'd held previously. But the syndicate had its drug traffic thoroughly organized, until the recent crackdowns. All our friends had to do was put trusted agents at key points along the line, to insert the materials they wanted transmitted into the drug containers, and take them out again. The syndicate then did all the work, unknowingly, of getting the stuff secretly into the country. As Martell said, Rizzi was running his errands for him."

I said, "It seems kind of like using a man-eating tiger for pony-rides at the fair."

"They probably only used the route for critical and difficult transmissions like this one. But when they

wanted it, it was there." I heard him clear his throat—
warning me that we were returning to the subject I had
so subtly shelved, I thought. "As I say, Eric, it doesn't
seem as if you've been operating at top efficiency."

"I could claim personal involvement and inadequate
briefing," I said, "but I won't. Guilty on counts a) and b).
As for c) I told them they were under arrest, as you
more or less instructed me to do. They just didn't seem
to believe me. Maybe I didn't speak with enough convic-
tion. I haven't had much practice at arresting people,
sir."

"It's a point, but not a very good one," he said. "Maybe
you need a rest, Eric. As a matter of fact, I just happen
to know a place . . . You like fishing, don't you? Well,
as soon as you're released from the hospital, get your fishing tackle and . . ."

It was a lake up in the mountains, never mind where,
and there never was a more ideal place to convalesce from
a bullet wound, to hear him tell it.

"Yes, sir," I said. "It sounds swell. Thank you very
much, sir."

He said, "You can stay on into the hunting season, if
you like. In fact, I'd suggest bringing a heavy rifle along,
preferably with a telescopic sight . . . oh, and some pistol
ammunition, of course, so that you can keep in practice."

"Practice," I said. "Yes, sir. You don't think I should
take along a bazooka or a small mountain howitzer as
well?"

"I shouldn't think that would be necessary," he said, but
I noticed he didn't sound quite sure. "Well, good-bye, Eric.
Take care of yourself."

It looked as if I'd have to. It was a cinch he wasn't
going to. I put the phone back and leaned against the
pillows and thought about the lake up in the mountains.
I wondered what Mac had lost up there and what I'd
have to do to find it. . . .